Falling for the Nanny

JACQUELINE DIAMOND

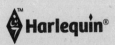

TORONTO NEW YORK LONDON
AMSTERDAM PARIS SYDNEY HAMBURG
STOCKHOLM ATHENS TOKYO MILAN MADRID
PRAGUE WARSAW BUDAPEST AUCKLAND

Recycling programs
for this product may
not exist in your area.

ISBN-13: 978-0-373-75362-8

FALLING FOR THE NANNY

ABOUT THE AUTHOR

The author of more than eighty-five romances and mysteries, Jacqueline Diamond developed an interest in police and security issues while working as a reporter for a newspaper and the Associated Press. Her interest in medical issues began when she was born—her father, then the only doctor in Menard, Texas, delivered her at home. She later successfully underwent fertility treatments to give birth to two sons, both now in their twenties (and both born in hospitals). Jackie and her husband, Kurt, live in Orange County, California. She hopes you'll visit her website at www.jacquelinediamond.com to get the latest on her books and writing tips.

Books by Jacqueline Diamond

HARLEQUIN AMERICAN ROMANCE

*Downhome Doctors
†Harmony Circle
**Safe Harbor Medical

To my outstanding editor, Kathleen Scheibling

Chapter One

Patty Hartman had almost everything she needed. She had a digital camera with high magnification, a spare cap to use as a disguise and a copy of today's newspaper with a hole in the middle. Through it, she was keeping an eye on forty-two-year-old former construction worker Stanley Frimley, who claimed that a severe on-the-job back injury had rendered him permanently handicapped.

A few houses down the block in this modest neighborhood of 1950s gingerbread homes, the fellow leaned heavily on his walker as he directed a gardener planting a bougainvillea. It was a lovely, peaceful scene washed by the May sunshine of the aptly named Safe Harbor, California.

Yes, she almost had it all. Sitting in her beat-up but reliable sedan with her camera at the ready, she thought about the one thing she didn't have and really, really needed.

A porta-potty.

Right now, she'd trade every man she'd ever loved and lost—grand total of one—for a portable potty. But that would have to wait because, in the yard, Stanley Frimley had started gesturing agitatedly at the gardener. She could read the guy's lips: *Needs to be closer to the fence... No, no, you idiot, not halfway across the yard!*

Whoa! The former surfer supposedly disabled by a fall on a construction site had just moved away from his walker and taken a step forward, angrily shaking his shaggy blond hair. Before she could switch on the video, though, the lying cheat had grabbed the walker and drooped over it like a plucked flower in the hot sun.

He hadn't winced in pain or wobbled in the slightest. On top of that, the veteran surfer still looked plenty muscular considering his allegedly debilitated state. But a single step and a buff physique weren't enough evidence to prove he was defrauding the insurance company.

Irritated, Patty settled back. One good thing about the near miss: for a few minutes, she'd forgotten her bladder. Surveillance was tough on women, but she refused to use gender as an excuse for anything. Ever since Alec Denny had dumped her in high school and broken her girlish heart, she'd straightened her spine and toughened up.

Around the corner, a black-and-white turned onto the street. A glow of recognition spread through Patty. For five years, until last month, one of those cruisers had been her second home. She and her partner, Leo, had poked into every corner of town while swapping wisecracks and catching lawbreakers.

As the car rolled by, the officer in the passenger seat glanced Patty's way, no doubt wondering why some woman was sitting in a car on a residential street. Not that there was anything noteworthy about her stick-straight blond hair or what little was visible of her stocky figure.

Suddenly, Bill Sanchez's gaze widened. He started to wave, caught her glare and subsided. Yeah, that would really help her cover, having Bill greet her like a long-lost buddy.

They rolled past. For a fleeting moment, Patty wished she was with them. Not that she'd expected private detective work to be like some fast-paced TV show, but jeez. Stanley Frimley was so boring that watching a guy plant a bougainvillea was the highlight of the past week.

Well, this was the new career she'd chosen. After losing out on a promotion, she'd accepted an offer from a detective she admired, Mike Aaron, to join Fact Hunter Investigations, the company he'd recently bought. Mike had a high opinion of her abilities, and Patty was determined to live up to it.

During the past week, between conducting employee background checks for a local medical-device manufacturing company, she'd grown increasingly frustrated while observing Stanley. One morning, hoping to get closer without drawing attention to herself, she'd borrowed a friend's dog and walked it around the block so many times it had started whining about sore paws. She'd heard clanking noises in Stanley's garage that sounded suspiciously like an exercise machine, but you couldn't produce that as evidence.

Back to the bougainvillea, which the gardener had finally wedged into what Stanley deemed to be the right spot. Too close to the fence, in Patty's opinion, because as the little plant beefed up it was going to thrust its elbows in every direction. But that wasn't her problem.

As the workman packed down the soil, Stanley swung around. To Patty's dismay, his gaze fixed on her and a frown creased his brow.

She'd been spotted.

Now what? Pretend to be a Realtor examining the house for sale across the street? Nah. Time to cut her losses.

Putting the car in gear, Patty slipped on her sunglasses and pulled away. Although she avoided looking directly at the guy, she could feel him watching.

Maybe she should give up for today. What a relief to head to the nearest public restroom, at a supermarket two blocks away.

Problem was, Stanley didn't often venture into public view. If he ran true to form, he'd go back into his house and stay there until his twice-weekly foray to the store, driving an

SUV with a blue handicap placard. Not only was the guy a low-down phony, but he was forcing old ladies with heart conditions to trundle down long parking lanes while he stole their reserved spaces.

She had to stop him, and this might be her best shot.

Out of sight around the corner, Patty pulled to the curb. After shedding her blue blazer to reveal a plain T-shirt, she tucked her hair into a gray baseball cap. She was already wearing running shoes, so she was covered there. Quickly, she checked her appearance in the rearview mirror. Nearly thirty, but she could pass for twenty-five and maybe younger if you didn't look too closely.

She'd never been the girlie type. Apparently that was what Alec preferred, because according to gossip, he'd married an exotic beauty who could pass for a model. That was the problem with growing up in a small town: you couldn't help hearing about your ex, even when you'd rather not. Like the news that he was back in town, setting up some kind of lab at the hospital. Well, so what?

Ignoring her body's demands, she freed her almost brand-new skateboard from the trunk and set off. Better hurry. No telling when Stanley would go scuttling back into his shell.

Must be hard on the guy, Patty mused as she zipped past a cheery bed of geraniums. According to his background report, Stanley used to enjoy sports like snowboarding, dirt biking and motocross, as well as surfing. He'd had to give all those up—at least when anyone might be looking.

Had to give them all up for a lifetime of free money that he didn't deserve.

Ahead, as the gardener's truck rolled away, Stanley stood staring after it. His hands tightened on the walker and he rocked back and forth, jaw working. Longing for freedom from his self-imposed restraint?

Patty did a couple of hard pushes to work up speed. His head turned—good, he was looking at her—*go for it!*

She slammed her foot on the back of the board and snapped a quick ollie jump to whet his appetite. Better not overdo it, or he might start wondering why she was so intent on performing tricks in front of him. Then she deliberately lost the board, landed smoothly and grabbed it off his lawn, where she pretended to examine it for scratches. Well, not entirely pretending.

"Kind of a fancy board for a beginner," the man sniped.

"It's my brother's." Patty hated lying. Except to scumbags. "Great graphics, huh?" She indicated the cartoon cop with flames spurting from his 9 mm.

Stanley shrugged. Weird to see him up close, after observing from a distance for the past week. "I've got two boards better than that," he boasted.

"I bet you're awesome." She wasn't sure whether that passed for flirting, which had never been Patty's strong point, but he seemed to buy it. "What happened to you, anyway?"

"Construction accident."

"Tough break." She held the board upright, so loosely it nearly slipped from her grasp.

"Watch it!" Stanley grabbed the edge. "Your brother must be nuts, letting a freaking amateur like you borrow this."

If this was the man's idea of how to talk to women, no wonder he still lived alone in his forties. Patty still lived alone, too, but that was different.

Because I choose it.

Since flirting hadn't worked, she shifted to goading. "You're too old for stuff like this, anyway," she jeered. "What're you, sixty?"

That did it. "Idiot," he muttered, and grabbed the board. "Watch how it's *supposed* to be done."

A thunk on the sidewalk, a rumble of wheels and he was

off. Pulling her camera from her back pocket, Patty started taping. Flying in the opposite direction, throwing in a flip trick along the way, he didn't notice, so she eased back to get the abandoned walker into the frame.

Problem: his face didn't show. And he'd just whizzed out of sight around the corner.

She listened hard. Was he turning to head back or was he circling the block? She heard nothing but the murmur of a passing delivery van, the tweeting of some love-besotted bird and the angst-hyped voices from an afternoon soap opera drifting through a neighbor's window. At last she caught the clatter of wheels on concrete and then he came bombing around the opposite bend, digging in on the toe edge to make the board turn sharply, showing off his skill.

Patty caught it all. His thin face. The long, stringy hair. His plaid shirt unbuttoned over the belly to reveal a stomach-churning amount of hair.

"Hey!" He spotted the camera. "You can't video me!"

"But you're way cool! You'll be a sensation on YouTube!" She winced, registering that she'd overdone the gee-whiz act.

He halted in front of her and hopped off. "Wait a minute. You're the woman from the car."

"What car?"

"You're a detective, damn you!"

Patty cut off the video and backed away. "Aw, come on. I caught you fair and square." Common sense dictated she should leave now. It was foolish to risk a confrontation, and Patty hated screwing up. Wanted to be the best, damn it.

But she loved that skateboard. She'd custom-designed it herself on the internet.

The jerk stood there, gripping it and taunting, "Trade you for the camera."

"No way!"

"I just want to delete what you shot. Scout's honor."

"No deal. Sorry." Dangerous moment. The guy had at least fifty pounds on her and he was ticked off. Unless he pulled a weapon, though, Patty refused to give up.

"You're going to be sorry, all right." He flexed his arm muscles.

She decided to try logic. "Don't you think you have enough problems without adding an assault and robbery rap, Mr. Frimley?"

"My only problem is you."

"Getting into a fight isn't going to help your claim of being disabled."

He was thinking that over, an obviously laborious process, so she grabbed the board. "Thanks." She flung it down, jumped on it and pushed off.

For a scary second, she thought he might give chase. That she'd end up bruised and sprawled across the sidewalk, camera gone, and that she'd have let down Mike. Then, across the street, a woman stepped outside and paused, key in hand, to stare at them.

A witness. Excellent.

By the time Patty had wedged the board in the backseat, jumped into the car and started up, Stanley was retreating into his house with the aid of the walker. Trying to salvage what he could of his pathetic cover, as if there was anything left to salvage.

One more duty: Patty pulled up across the street, found the witness and made a note of her name and phone number. The woman said she'd be happy to talk later, but she was on her way out, running late to a doctor's appointment.

That was okay with Patty. She was finally free to drive to the supermarket.

WHOSE BRILLIANT IDEA was it to locate the new embryology laboratory in the basement of Safe Harbor Medical Center?

Alec Denny wondered as he finished reviewing the contractor's latest report. It summed up the progress they'd made installing a specialized water filtration system, which would clear the water of both organic and inorganic substances before it was used in embryo development.

That lab and several others being assembled under his supervision lay an inconvenient elevator ride from his office here on the fifth floor, and a not-much-more-convenient ride from the egg-retrieval rooms on the second floor. Oh, and he'd better not forget the fertility program support services, which had been given a suite on the first floor.

It amazed him that the new program's director, world-renowned fertility specialist Dr. Owen Tartikoff, had agreed to leave his longtime base in Boston for such an awkward setup. According to reports, the hospital had originally intended to convert a nearby dental building, but the sale had fallen through. Surely it would have been better to wait until another separate structure could be acquired rather than stick the program's components into odds and ends of available space.

And yet Alec was glad to be back in Safe Harbor. The seaside town, located in Orange County about an hour's drive south of Los Angeles, had parks and a beach, as well as a harbor filled with sailboats and yachts. It was small enough to be friendly and large enough to offer excellent schools.

After the turmoil of his divorce and custody battle, Alec appreciated the chance to put distance between his four-year-old daughter and her volatile mother. Being near Grandma Darlene would provide Fiona with the stability she deserved, in the community where he'd grown up.

Frankly, he'd have moved to Antarctica if that's what it took to protect his little girl. He had let her down once. He'd never risk that again.

A tap at the door announced the presence of the hospital

administrator, Dr. Mark Rayburn. Built like a football player, the guy struck Alec as a gentle giant. His even temperament provided a much-needed counterbalance to Owen's hard-driving and sometimes caustic personality. Although Alec had developed a smooth working relationship with Dr. T. over the past four years, he was glad for the chance to arrive in advance to get the lab up and running without having to explain and justify every decision.

"How's it going?" Mark asked. "On schedule, I hope."

The fertility program's opening was set for September, although they'd be seeing patients informally before then. The hospital, which had been remodeled in recent years to specialize in maternity and other women's medical issues, already had a number of obstetricians on staff.

"Things are right on track." Alec leaned back in the swivel chair and glanced out his window. In the distance, he caught a glimpse of the Pacific Ocean, a reminder of lazy childhood summers when his path through life had seemed clear-cut.

"How're you settling in? Relocating from the East Coast can't be easy on you and your daughter." Mark lingered in the doorway. Alec would have offered him a seat, but so far his office furniture didn't include a guest chair. "You must have a few old friends around here, though."

"Aside from my mother, I haven't stayed in touch with anyone." Especially not Patty, the girl he'd once loved. He'd heard from Darlene that she'd become a police officer, and didn't look forward to the inevitable moment when he ran into her again. At the very least, she'd probably slap him with a ticket.

"You haven't run into any classmates? Seems like half our staff graduated from Safe Harbor High."

"Now that you mention it, yes. Several." When one former schoolmate, a nurse, had invited him to accompany her to an upcoming wedding, Alec had agreed as a friendly gesture.

She didn't seem to consider it a date; mostly, she was eager to talk about her efforts to get pregnant as a surrogate for her sister. It was amazing how much private information women divulged when they discovered he was an embryologist. The fact that he had a PhD rather than an MD didn't seem to dissuade them.

"I'm sure you'll fit in," the administrator said. "Let me know if there's anything I can do."

"Absolutely."

As Mark departed, Alec's phone jingled with a melody that sent him on full alert. It belonged to Fiona's nanny, who'd moved with them from Boston. She almost never called unless it was urgent. "Tatum. Anything wrong?"

"Fiona's fine," she reassured him. Judging by the background noise, she was calling from her car. He'd made sure she had a hands-free phone, in accordance with California law. "It's your mom."

That jolted him. At fifty-eight, Darlene was an active community volunteer and a force of nature. He'd never worried about her health. "Is she all right?"

"At the park, she fell off the monkey bars and hurt her ankle." Playing with Fiona, obviously. How typical of his mother. "We're not sure if it's sprained or broken. I'm taking her to the doctor."

Faintly, he heard a voice call, "Tell my son not to worry. I'll be fine."

And another voice: "Is that Daddy? Hi, Daddy!"

A surge of tenderness flooded Alec. He'd never imagined he could love anyone so intensely or completely as he had from the moment he'd first held his daughter in his arms. "How can I help?" he asked Tatum.

"Her doctor's in the medical building next to the hospital. I'm sure he'll want X-rays, and her housekeeper's out sick again, so I should stay with her." For a twenty-three-year-old, the nanny was highly responsible. "Fiona's likely to get bored. Any chance you could take her?"

While Alec didn't like to leave the office early on a Thursday afternoon, he could read reports at home tonight. And if his daughter needed him, even to save her from a few hours of restless tedium, he'd be there. "You bet. I'll meet you in front of the office building."

"See you in a couple of minutes."

Before he could click off, his mother announced, "We're out of milk and breakfast cereal, and we could use a dozen eggs. Oh, and a loaf of bread." She lived downstairs in the same condo building, so they often shared meals.

"I'll pick them up on the way home," Alec promised.

"See you in a few," Tatum said.

"Bye, Daddy!" called the voice that always wrapped a warm blanket around his heart.

"Bye, sweetheart." Although his words probably went into Tatum's ear rather than Fiona's, he couldn't resist answering.

Alec packed his gear and made his way out. To the temp secretary holding down the fort, he explained that he was leaving for the day but reachable on his cell.

He took the stairs, since climbing up and down those five flights often constituted his main form of daily exercise. On the first floor, Alec caught a whiff of grilled meat from the cafeteria, and added a roast chicken for dinner to his mental grocery list.

Exiting through the staff door, he strode along the walkway between the two buildings, past flower beds brimming with pink and purple petunias. The air carried a hint of ocean brine.

Alec had loved Boston's intellectual ferment and the sense of being surrounded by history while feeling vitally involved in the future. Coming back to Southern California was like touring a past that belonged to someone else. Of course, he'd visited his parents on occasion, and had helped arrange his father's funeral two years ago, but the trips had been tightly scheduled affairs. He'd deliberately skipped his ten-year high school reunion.

In the weeks since his return, Alec hadn't had much of a chance to slow down and breathe the salt air. He was almost glad events had conspired to give him an afternoon alone with his daughter—not that he would have wished Darlene an injury.

Climbing on the monkey bars. She'd certainly changed since his own childhood days.

Ahead, he spotted a threesome emerging from the parking garage. Darlene Denny was limping as she leaned on the taller, thinner nanny. Then a little girl skipped into view from behind them, her light-brown hair woven into a thick braid like Tatum's.

"Daddy! Daddy!" She pelted down the walkway, straight into Alec's arms. He whirled her around, relishing the solid feel of her little body and the delicious way her face burrowed into his neck.

"Hey, pumpkin. Kind of rough on your grandma today, huh?" he teased.

"She hurt her ankle." Fiona clung to him.

He carried her to meet his mother and the nanny. "Mom, you don't need to walk. You could have gotten out right in front of the building."

"I offered to let her off," Tatum told him.

"Nonsense." Darlene grimaced. "It's only a bruise."

"Tatum, thanks for handling this." Alec couldn't help noticing a hint of strain on the nanny's face. She'd done him and Fiona a huge favor by relocating, leaving behind friends and family, and now she was going way beyond her job description.

Although Tatum got regular time off—when Alec happened to be tied up on an evening or weekend, his mother handled babysitting duties—the housekeeper he shared with Darlene had been ill a lot lately. Often one of her nieces filled in, but when they weren't available, Tatum grabbed a vacuum and set to work, despite Alec's urging that she leave the chores to him.

"I'm glad you can spend a few hours with Fiona. She's been restless today." The young woman guided Darlene toward the automatic door. "I guess we'll see you when we see you."

"I'll have dinner ready." He shifted his grip on Fiona, who still hung on him. "You okay to walk, cutie, or are you crippled like Grandma?"

His mother laughed, and Fiona wiggled to the ground so fast he nearly lost his balance. "Let's go, Daddy. Can we buy ice cream?"

"The low-sugar kind," Tatum warned.

"Got it."

His mother and the nanny disappeared into the building. Holding tight to his little girl's hand, Alec walked her to his reserved space on the lower floor of the garage. There, he strapped her into the booster seat in the back.

Grocery shopping with a child, he reflected as he put the engine in gear, wasn't a simple toss-it-in-the-cart-and-check-out procedure. When he was in a hurry, it could be frustrating.

Today, though, shopping with Fiona felt like an adventure. He looked forward to it.

Chapter Two

To lure upscale shoppers, the recently remodeled Suncrest Supermarket greeted customers with a vibrant array of cut flowers and mounded displays of fresh peaches, tomatoes, cherries and watermelons. The meandering pathway between bins, no doubt intended to encourage a leisurely pace, merely annoyed Patty.

If she had her way, stores would put their bathrooms right in front, possibly in large kiosks by the check stands. And they wouldn't clutter the aisles with cardboard displays of specialty items. Who needed a slicer-dicer-ricer anyway?

Ahead, she gauged that she could just squeeze between a couple of older women examining the English muffins. Beyond them, in a cart, a small girl sat swinging her legs and complaining, "Daddy! I need to go potty!"

"That makes two of us," Patty muttered as she angled past. She didn't realize she'd spoken aloud until a man, apparently the kid's father, turned from the shelves with a loaf of bread in hand and said, "Fiona, can't you wait a—?" And broke off abruptly.

Time stopped. The rattle of carts, the buzz of voices and the canned music faded. Patty was seventeen again, one big raw throbbing wound, gazing into the milk-chocolate eyes of Alec Denny as he told her that, after three and a half years together, he was breaking up with her. It had been right after the homecoming dance, and she hadn't believed him at first. She'd thought it must be a joke.

Now here he stood a dozen years later, the intense boy having matured into a heart-stopping sculpture of a man— *stop exaggerating, Patty*—okay, a well-built guy with thick hair that barely stopped short of his eyes, and an expression that could melt and scald her at the same time.

"Oh, hey, Alec. Long time no see," she said. "Sorry, gotta run."

"Patty! Thank goodness. I could really use your help."

That stopped her. She hated letting anyone down. Even Alec.

"I can't take my little girl in the men's room. I mean, I could, but it doesn't seem right." He lifted the kid out of the cart. A cute child with brown hair and an elfin face, she looked as if she could stir up her share of mischief. "Would you mind? I know it's a lot to ask, but I'd really appreciate it."

The tot in question hopped up and down on the linoleum, squealing, "I gotta go *now!*"

"Fiona, this is Daddy's old friend Patty." He gazed at her appealingly. "Please?"

Patty had never spent much time around kids, and she never knew what to say to them. But it was faster to yield than to argue. "Sure." She grabbed the child's hand. "Come on."

They made a break for it, dodging carts and skimming around displays. By some miracle, the ladies' room had a pair of stalls available. Patty figured Fiona was too old for diapers, but beyond that she had no idea what to do. It was true she had a sister six years younger, named Rainbow courtesy of their ditzy parents, but she and her brother, Drew, had grown up with their ex-military grandfather, a mechanic nicknamed the Sergeant after his former rank. To earn pocket money, she'd mowed lawns and cleaned out garages rather than babysitting.

"You need any help?" she asked.

Fiona's face scrunched in disgust. "I'm nearly five!"

"Great," said Patty, and dodged into one of the stalls.

She emerged to find the little girl scrubbing her hands at a sink. Patty gave her own a quick once-over.

"You didn't do it long enough."

"Excuse me?" She paused, wrists in the air, dripping water.

"To kill the germs," the child declared. "You have to sing 'Twinkle Twinkle Little Star' all the way through."

"Every time you wash?" Again, figuring it was easier to comply than complain, Patty stuck her hands under the faucet. "What's your mom, some kind of clean freak?"

"My dad's a 'bryologist," Fiona announced proudly. "That's a scientist."

"What's your mom do?"

The child's forehead puckered. "I don't know."

"Does she stay home with you?" While being a full-time mom was Patty's idea of extreme boredom, she respected individuals who made that choice. *If the world were full of women like me, the human race would be in big trouble.*

"No. She doesn't live with us."

"Your folks are divorced?"

"Yeah."

Now, there was a surprise. What had gone wrong between Alec and his beautiful bride? Sabrina, that was her name. Patty had heard her praised by a classmate who'd met her through Darlene Denny. But that had been quite a while ago.

Divorce must be tough on the kid. It seemed odd that the father had custody, though. "How come you live with Daddy?"

Patty blurted, before reflecting that interrogating a four-year-old on her family situation might not be appropriate.

"My mom is unstable."

That didn't sound like the kind of remark a child would make. "Who told you that?"

"Grandma."

Hmmm. Apparently the perfect wife hadn't scored such a hit with Darlene, after all. While that might say more about Grandma's rigid standards than it did about the younger woman, Patty sympathized with the little girl caught in the middle. "So, who takes care of you all day?"

"Tatum."

"And she is…?" Might as well finish satisfying her curiosity, since Alec had sent her blithely off with this tiny fountain of information.

"My nanny. She took Grandma to the doctor," Fiona explained. "Okay, you washed your hands enough."

"Right." They were getting chapped, but it had been worth it.

They found Alec waiting for them outside the restroom. If only her gut didn't do this instinctive lurch when she spotted him, Patty thought, and her brain didn't pop out a memory of a day umpteen years ago when they'd gone grocery shopping together for a beach picnic. She hadn't paid much attention to what they'd put in the cart. All she'd been able to think about was plunging through the surf with him, playfully tussling in their skimpy swimsuits and then getting him alone after the sun went down….

"Everything all right?" he asked.

"She did great," Patty told him. "Made me scrub the skin off my hands. Guess that's your influence."

He beamed at Patty in a loopy way. "She bossed *you* around? That's amazing."

"Why?" Fiona grasped the handle on the cart and gave it a push.

"Did Patty tell you what she does for a living?" Alec halted the cart inches from a display of spaghetti sauce. "She's a police officer."

Now, where had he heard about that? "Well, until a month ago."

Placing his hands outside his daughter's on the bar, he helped guide the cart as they lurched toward the checkout. "What happened a month ago?"

"A friend of mine bought a detective agency and I decided to give it a try," she told him. "I got passed over for a promotion, which was fine, because my partner, Leo, deserved it. But I didn't like the idea of patrolling with anybody else, and I needed a challenge."

That wasn't the whole story. The truth was, she'd let herself down by not pursuing the promotion hard enough. *If you don't develop more ambition, girl, you'll end up a mess like your parents.* How many times had Grandpa said that?

"So you're a detective." He sent her an amused grin. "In a T-shirt and jeans?"

She hadn't bothered to put the blazer back on, although she *had* removed the cap. "I nailed an insurance cheat just a few minutes ago." As they reached the check stand, it occurred to Patty that the other shoppers probably figured the three of them were a family. Man, woman, kid, cart full of food. How strange to think that if they hadn't broken up, they might actually be… Nope. Not worth thinking about.

"Nailed a guy?" Alec repeated.

She pulled out her camera. "I'll show you." When she was with the force, she'd never have revealed evidence, and she didn't intend to provide any identifying information. But that scene with Stanley begged to be shared.

"Can I see?" Fiona demanded.

"You bet." As she got the video running, Patty realized that while she was at the market, she, too, should buy something for dinner. Well, no point in making a fuss about it, when they sold candy bars right at the counter.

ALEC COULDN'T REMEMBER when he'd laughed so hard. Man, that was funny, the shaggy cheater zooming up on the skateboard and realizing he'd been outed.

Then anger flashed across the guy's narrow face. Suddenly Alec didn't feel like laughing. "He might have attacked you."

"Yeah." Patty turned off the camera. "Kind of a tense moment there. But he just mouthed off a little."

"Did you arrest the bad man?" Fiona asked.

"Private detectives don't arrest people," Patty explained. "I'll write up a report and copy the video for the insurance agency. They'll take it from there."

"Won't he go to jail? He's committed fraud," Alec said.

She shrugged. "Somebody would have to report this to the police, and we leave that to our client. I expect they'll use the possibility of criminal charges as leverage to make him drop his claim and repay the money he's received. That's all they really want."

To Alec, she seemed to be dismissing the danger too easily. "That leaves this guy running around loose. What if he spots you on the street and decides to take revenge?"

Her chin came up, a familiar motion he'd seen countless times in high school when she was dead set on pursuing some escapade. He'd never been able to resist joining her. "Then I might have to teach him a lesson."

"Are you a teacher?" Fiona gave the cart a shove to keep up with the line.

"I teach lessons to grown-ups who forget their manners."

Patty indicated the carton of eggs wedged in the cart. "And I hear your daddy's really good with eggs."

"He makes omelets," Fiona agreed.

"She's referring to what I do for a living," Alec told her.

"You make babies for lots and lots of mommies!" his daughter proclaimed, loudly enough for people in the adjacent lines to turn and stare.

He flushed. "That's right."

"I'll bet you make lots and lots of mommies happy and satisfied," Patty added at approximately the same volume.

Alec considered poking her in the ribs, but decided against it. "That's my job, all right."

They'd reached the conveyer belt. She set down a couple of chocolate bars, stuck a rubber divider in place and watched as Alex began unloading his groceries. "Ice cream, yeah. Glad to see you didn't waste your money on fruits and vegetables."

He felt a guilty twinge. "My mother didn't mention those."

Patty's forehead puckered. "Fiona said your mom had to go to the doctor. Is she all right?"

"Injured her ankle. She fell off the monkey bars."

She stared at him. "Is this the same Mrs. Denny who glared at me for putting my feet on the coffee table?"

"I have only one mother." Alec had to admit, Darlene hadn't been thrilled at his choice of girlfriend. Now, after his fiasco of a marriage to a woman who'd initially charmed and dazzled his parents, he wondered if his mother had rethought her criteria.

Too late to do anything about that now. Running into Patty had been fun, but they'd both moved on, into different worlds. Or perhaps they'd always lived in different worlds and his teenage self simply hadn't noticed.

Fiona tugged his arm. "Daddy, can I have candy bars like Patty?"

"We already bought dessert." He indicated the ice cream.

Ahead of them, Patty handed the cashier a couple of bills. "I'm having these for dinner."

Fiona stared in awe. "Can you do that?"

"She's joking." Alec narrowed his eyes at Patty.

"Sorry. I forget I'm supposed to set a good example." To Fiona, she said, "I eat 'em fried, roasted and grilled with pepper sauce." She winked at the little girl. "See you."

Off she strolled, as if she hadn't a care in the world. Alec had never known anyone who lived as strongly in the moment as his old girlfriend.

"She's cool," Fiona said.

"Very cool," he conceded.

But he'd made a choice a dozen years ago, and even if he could go back, he wouldn't change it.

Chapter Three

Patty sang along with a golden oldie on the radio, "My Boy-friend's Back." How appropriate.

Seeing Alec again had been both sweet and bitter. Like candy bars with pepper sauce, she mused wryly. What a dar-ling little girl he had. If her mother was anything like her, what had gone wrong?

Patty might be tempted to take some satisfaction in the failure of even such a paragon of womanhood, but Sabrina Denny hadn't stolen Alec from her. Besides, a divorce meant pain for everyone involved.

Had he pulled the same 180-degree turn on his wife as he had on his high-school sweetheart? That dismissal out of nowhere—she certainly hadn't seen it coming—still burned. True, he'd been neglecting his studies, but so had she. They could have worked together to get back on track.

Old news. Get over it.

Fact Hunter Investigations was located above an escrow company and next to the Sexy Over Sixty Gym in a small shopping center on Lyons Way. The second-floor location, which at first had struck Patty as kind of low-rent, had a public relations advantage, according to Mike. The small percent-age of clients that actually dropped by the agency preferred to park in front of something neutral rather than a detective agency, in case anyone spotted their car. They'd rather not have their friends and neighbors guess that they suspected their spouse of cheating or their employees of embezzling.

Once you topped the flight of stairs, the place took on a sharp, professional air. Mike had added a fresh coat of paint and sturdy beige carpeting. His detective license stood out on one wall, along with a private patrol operator license that allowed them to do bodyguard and security work. These were surrounded by awards, commendations and certificates from special courses he'd completed while working as a detective for the Safe Harbor police.

Sue Carrera, the secretary who'd come with the place, was on the phone, speaking Spanish. Patty caught the words *esposo* and *mujer*—husband and woman. The language of faithless spouses was pretty much universal.

From an inner office emerged a tall, sandy-haired man, wearing a better suit than in his police detective days and a pair of glasses Patty hadn't seen before. "What's with the specs?"

Mike gave the tiniest of starts, which was unusual, because he rarely got caught off guard. "Didn't hear you come in."

"Must be my catlike grace," she told him. "Hey, I nailed Frimley. Wanna see a hilarious video?"

"Climbing a ladder?" he guessed.

"Skateboarding!" Stepping into the office, she ran the video for him.

Mike responded with a rolling chuckle. "Good work, Pats."

His approval rippled through her the way her grandpa's used to on those rare occasions when she rose to his high standards. Patty was glad she'd never felt any romantic stirrings toward Mike, even when he'd helped her try to land the promotion. Although he was good-looking and in his early thirties, she valued his critical approval too much to date him.

"Don't you love the way he started to show off for the camera before it hit him what I was doing?" she said, extending the moment.

"It made my day." Mike adjusted his glasses, which he still hadn't explained.

"Is that a disguise?" she blurted. "You're too young for reading glasses."

He tucked them into his shirt pocket. "My vision gets blurry from the computer glare. I spent most of the morning running background checks."

"I'm glad you assign me the fun stuff."

"Speaking of which, I have another case for you." He handed her a printout sheet from his desk. "A Mr. and Mrs. Finnegan discovered their eighteen-year-old daughter's been trolling for men on the internet. She's set up a meeting they'd like you to monitor. At a local restaurant."

Patty glanced at the sheet. "Saturday? I'm in Leo's wedding, remember?" Although she was hardly the bridesmaid type, she'd been flattered when her partner's fiancée, Dr. Nora Kendall, had asked her to be the maid of honor. Patty hadn't put on a dress since her high school homecoming dance, and didn't intend to, so, after some good-natured negotiations, they'd settled on her wearing a tuxedo.

"I'll cover Saturday's rendezvous. You can take it from there. Wish we weren't so short-handed." Mike had been counting on his foster brother and coinvestor, an Arizona sheriff's deputy named Lock Vaughn, joining them. The guy had managed to get himself shot in the leg and was temporarily out of commission.

Patty hated disappointing Mike, even though he didn't seem to mind. "I guess we're a bit too busy."

"Seems like it, but most of these cases can be wrapped up in no time." Mike sat on the edge of his broad desk, its surface covered by neatly stacked files and notes lined up side by side. "As you know, we inherited some large corporate clients, but they won't pay all the bills. We get hits on our website and through the Yellow Pages, but those aren't enough, either. Anything you can do to help bring in cases would be appreciated."

"Me?" Patty hadn't considered getting involved in the marketing end of the business, but while this was Mike and Lock's company, she had a stake here, too. "I could nose around at the wedding. You should come, too. I'll bet you could make it in time for the reception." Although the affair was a small one, Patty was allowed to bring a guest.

"That's a good idea from a business standpoint. Nora's got connections at the hospital, and Leo's family is prominent in this town." Mike rubbed his forehead. "Okay, if I finish in time, I'll be there."

"Just show up and say you're with me." She scanned the sheet again. "The meeting's at one. Wedding doesn't start till four. I can do both."

"You're the maid of honor."

"It's not like I have to arrive three hours early. Nora said half an hour would be fine."

"You certain about this?"

I'm sure I want to carry my weight around here. "You have to admit, Miss Finnegan's a lot less likely to notice a woman spying on her than a big guy like you." Patty had another thought. "You got an ID on this Romeo? If he's a sex offender, we could have a police escort waiting for him."

Mike shook his head. "Nothing yet. Besides, the girl's eighteen. She can meet anybody she likes. You sure you want to do this?"

"No question." Patty checked her watch. "I'd better go write up the miraculous recovery of Mr. Frimley."

"Don't let me stop you."

She chose the private office set aside for Lock over the

report-writing room jammed with file cabinets and supplies. Feet happily propped on the desk of a detective she had yet to meet, Patty called Frimley's neighbor, who proved to be a gold mine. She'd actually seen Stanley working out in his garage once—the doors had opened on their own, before he'd managed to shut them again—and she provided names and phone numbers of a couple of other neighbors, as well.

After calling them and garnering a few more helpful observations, Patty set to work organizing her material. Even with the neighbors' testimony and the video as evidence, a careful recounting of facts was essential. The attorney for the other side could spin doubts around the smallest inconsistency.

Time of day. Weather. License plate of the gardener. She'd long ago trained herself to commit items like that to memory.

She hadn't seen any kids around, Patty recalled. At that hour, when she was growing up, she'd have been outdoors flying around on a bike or skates. Were they all stuck in day care, or glued to their video games, or what?

She wondered if Fiona was allowed to roam outside unsupervised. You didn't have to tell an ex-cop about the safety issues, but that curious, active little girl must ache to spread her wings and go exploring.

If she were my daughter, I'd find a way to give her as much independence as I could. Safely, of course.

Wait a minute. This couldn't be a sign of latent maternal instincts, could it? Patty's fingers hesitated over the keys. Sure, she liked Fiona, but she wasn't about to turn into somebody's mother.

On the other hand, as she'd reflected earlier, there was no telling what course her life might have taken if she and Alec had stayed together.

He used to kiss like nobody's business. Patty had never met another man who managed to be so gentle and so passionate at the same time. Holding her that special way, teasing her, then forgetting himself and…well, they hadn't quite done it in high school, but she felt certain they'd have gone all the way in senior year, if they hadn't broken up.

His parents had probably been worried about that. Sex, and the pernicious influence of a girl who too often preferred fun to academics. They'd given him an ultimatum as he prepared to send out his college applications. If he wanted their financial support, he needed to lose the girlfriend.

Patty had to admit she shouldn't have invited Alec to a party the night before he took the SATs. He'd surprised her by tossing back a couple of drinks, which was unusual for him. She'd learned later that he'd woken up the next day with a pounding headache, and his results had come in lower than expected.

He'd taken the tests again a few months later and scored much higher, but by then his parents had demanded he drop her. Knowing he was facing a long haul to either medical school or a PhD, Alec had caved rather than run up huge debts. Besides, he'd told Patty earnestly, high-school romances hardly ever lasted. In his view, the two of them were just bowing to the inevitable.

The day he'd broken the news, she'd felt sucker punched. For weeks, she hadn't believed he would stick to it. She'd moped by the phone, sat alone at lunch hoping he'd join her, even driven by his house trying to catch sight of him. Then her younger brother ratted her out to Grandpa.

His words still stung. "That boy's not worthy of you. Don't be one of those soft women who're always forgiving the men who wrong them."

Ashamed to have disappointed her grandfather, Patty had reined in her emotions and focused on her own grades. The day she was admitted to Cal State Long Beach's criminal justice program had been a triumph.

Her grandfather had been right and so had Alec. High-school love stories lasted only in the movies.

ON SATURDAY, Patty arrived an hour early at the designated coffee shop and circled it, noting the cars and license plates. If this guy was legitimate, he'd simply drive up at the appointed time. But the more she'd read the material supplied by Mrs. Finnegan, and checked the online databases to which the agency subscribed, the more suspicious she'd become.

Lover boy had given his name as Glenn Jerome and said he lived in Safe Harbor, but she couldn't find any records under that name. He also claimed to be twenty-five, and that he'd dropped out of college to pursue his dream of becoming a rock singer. Very romantic, but why couldn't she find any music videos of his?

The client's daughter, Judi, sounded very naive in her emails. She wrote about her plans to become a physical thera-pist, her volunteer work at a local hospital and her hopes of finding Mr. Right. While she'd had the sense not to give out her home address and phone number, data like that was easy to come by.

In the photo he'd sent, Glenn had cropped blond hair—not very rock-star-like, to Patty's way of thinking—and a sly smile. No way to tell when it had been shot, and of course it might not be him at all. Judi had sent a high-school picture that showed a friendly round face. He'd asked for something more personal, So I cn see how pretty u r all ovr.

She'd stalled, saying you never knew where images might end up, and also declined his request to switch to text mes-sages. Glenn hadn't been too happy about that, or about not being able to call her cell phone, but he'd given in.

It all seemed a little strange, Patty reflected as she found a parking spot with a clear view of the restaurant's entrance. If the Finnegans would just sit down and talk to their daughter, they might be able to clear up the whole business and send this guy packing. But then Fact Hunter Investigations would be minus one paying client.

It wasn't only liars and cheats that kept detectives in business. It was also people who had no idea how to communicate with their loved ones.

FIONA CHEWED HER CHICKEN sandwich slowly, her little face scrunched in deep thought. Well, deep thought for a four-year-old. Why couldn't she enjoy her lunch and the gorgeous view from their condo's balcony? Below the bluffs, colorful umbrellas dotted a pristine beach. Gulls wheeled, sailboats skimmed the sea and sunbathers worked on their tans despite the cool ocean air. Alec's daughter ignored them all.

"Daddy, a person *could* eat a chocolate bar for dinner if she really wanted to, couldn't she?" she said plaintively, revisiting the topic that had obsessed her for the past two days.

"Honey, no sane person would make a meal out of anything that unhealthy." Realizing his words might come back to haunt him, he amended that to, "Patty's a detective. I'm sure there are times when she's stuck on a job and has to stave off hunger pangs. She only eats them out of necessity."

"I get hunger pangs," his daughter responded.

Alec wondered what would happen if he allowed Fiona to try dining on chocolate bars one night until her teeth hurt. That might cure her. Or backfire. Worst case: his ex-wife could find out and use it against him.

"If you're hungry, eat your corn and peas," he said with what he considered irrefutable logic.

"I'm cold," Fiona countered.

The sea breeze *was* chilly, and while eating outside ought to be a fun experience, the endless rumble of the surf threatened to drown their voices. "Okay." Alec slid open the door, scooped up their plates and his glass and led the way inside. Fiona trailed him with the silverware and her spill-proof cup.

Tatum was frying a couple of eggs in the kitchen, which lay open to the informal dining area and large living room. "Too cold?"

"You got that right."

"Smells scrummy!" That was Fiona's word for scrumptious and yummy.

"Want some eggs?" the nanny asked.

"Yes, please!" Fiona set her load on the center island and ran to the woman who'd anchored her life for the past two years.

"It's your day off," Alec reminded Tatum.

"I don't mind." She gave the little girl a squeeze.

In Boston, the nanny had spent her days with Fiona but had shared an apartment with her two sisters, and Alec had been relieved when she'd agreed to move with them to California. She'd said she'd grown attached to his daughter, and had joked that everyone envied her the chance to live near the beach and escape the frosty New England winters. But, at least for now, the move also meant occupying Alec's third bedroom and being available to Fiona 24/7, despite Alec's efforts to protect her time off. The lack of privacy must be taking its toll.

"Well, you'll have the place to yourself this afternoon," he said as he set the lunch things on the table. His mother, whose ankle had turned out to be mildly sprained, would be hosting her granddaughter while he accompanied his former schoolmate to a wedding.

He almost wished he'd declined Bailey's invitation, but he wanted to get better acquainted with the bride, an obstetrician whom Bailey assisted. Nora Kendall had an ongoing disagreement with Dr. Tartikoff over how to handle her fertility patients, contending that, for some, the latest techniques were expensive and unnecessarily invasive. In Owen's view, moving full speed ahead boosted their chances of getting pregnant, and that justified the expense. He liked succeeding with patients, and a high rate of conception would enhance the program's reputation.

As part of Owen's team, Alec would prefer to see the new program get off to a smooth start. The wedding reception should present a great chance to socialize.

"I thought I'd check out the mall. I don't even own a decent swimsuit." Tatum slid the eggs onto Fiona's plate and set to frying a couple more for herself.

"How's your family?" He knew the nanny spent a lot of time texting her sisters and mother.

"Busy." She sounded wistful. "May's a beautiful month in Boston. The best time of the year. Except for fall, of course. Do the leaves change colors here?"

"The liquidambar trees do. And in spring, the jacarandas burst into lavender blooms. Haven't you noticed?"

"Not really." She sounded glum. "It's not much fun driving around by myself." Although Darlene allowed Tatum generous use of her car, the nanny stuck close to home.

"You'll make new friends."

"I guess."

His phone blared, the ring tone making Alec forget all about the nanny's loneliness. It played the Queen of the Night's furious aria from *The Magic Flute*.

His ex-wife was calling. Alec's hands tightened instinctively.

She'd endangered their daughter once. He'd been helpless then to protect Fiona, boxed in by the court's preliminary assumption that her mother was the best guardian for such a young child. If he'd known what would happen, he'd have defied the court. Now, given Sabrina's capricious nature and habit of picking fights, he might have to do battle again.

And he would. Whatever it cost.

Chapter Four

At about twelve-thirty, a battered pickup parked off to one side of the restaurant, out of view of the main windows. The man who got out bore little resemblance to the photo, but Patty had a feeling this might be him. Dirty-blond hair hung raggedly around his ears, and a glimpse of his profile showed a lip curling smugly. He swaggered as he crossed the lot in scuffed cowboy boots.

She took a few quick photos and wrote down his license number.

On her smartphone, she checked the database. The car was registered to a Glenn Jergens, not Glenn Jerome. Minor arrest record—breaking and entering, assault, receiving stolen property. No sex crimes. None that had been reported, anyway.

But if he was twenty-five, she was Miss America. And even without a major record, he could still be seriously dangerous. Although Patty knew the client's daughter only from a photograph, she felt a keen urge to shield her from this scumbag.

As more cars pulled in, Patty watched for the powder-blue compact the Finnegans had described. There it was, with Judi, as innocent looking as in her picture, at the wheel.

Two spaces from Patty's, a family with three youngsters piled out of their car. Under cover of the commotion, she slid out and followed Judi inside.

From a booth, Glenn Jergens signaled until he caught Judi's eye. He jutted his chin to gesture her over.

Be smart. Walk out.

The girl hesitated, although from behind Patty couldn't read her expression. Then she crossed to him.

As she approached, Judi lifted her cell phone and took his picture. Hmm. Now what was that about?

He didn't look too happy about it. There was a tense exchange of words and for a moment Patty expected the girl to leave. Instead, she took a seat across from him, talking in a wide-eyed, gushy manner.

Patty wasn't sure she believed the show of naiveté. But why would the girl try to manipulate this guy?

Although she'd have preferred a table with a good view of both Judi and Glenn, the only one fitting that description was directly in front of them. Too obvious. Instead, Patty chose a less conspicuous table from which she could clearly see the man and glimpse Judi's profile. She ordered a cup of coffee, took out a paperback murder mystery and settled down to pretend to read.

"ALL I'M ASKING IS TO SEE my daughter!" Sabrina's voice shrilled into Alec's ear. "You're the one who moved to the other side of the country. It isn't too much to ask that you put her and that nanny on a plane to visit me."

"Actually, it is."

Two years ago, the judge in their divorce had given Sabrina primary custody on a preliminary basis. Then a passerby had observed Fiona alone in a car and summoned the police. After learning that her mother had left her there for over an hour while visiting a boyfriend, the judge had awarded sole custody to Alec and allowed his ex only supervised visitation.

He'd had nightmares about what might have happened to his little girl while she sat by herself in a parking garage beneath an apartment building. Not quite three, she'd have been easy prey if an adult had ordered her to unlock the door. And what if, instead of dozing, she'd decided to go in search of Mommy?

As far as Alec was concerned, Sabrina was lucky to be allowed even supervised visits, and the nanny did not count as supervision. Wonderful as Tatum was, she had no authority to countermand Sabrina.

"You're welcome to come to California and spend a few days," he said tightly as he carried the phone down the hallway to his bedroom. "My mother and I will rearrange our schedules at your convenience." Reluctantly.

"That's not fair!" Sabrina's voice, so soothing and musical when she was in a good mood, cracked on a high note. "Eduardo has to return to Argentina for who knows how long. His wife is giving him trouble about the divorce! Naturally, I intend to go with him. I don't have time to run to the West Coast."

Eduardo Patron was Sabrina's fiancé—despite the fact that he remained married to the mother of his three children— and she was living with him in his New York penthouse. The nature of the man's business was somewhat murky to Alec, but apparently the Patron family owned a large manufacturing company.

He closed the door to the hall and hoped his little girl hadn't heard enough to upset her. "If you want to see Fiona, you'll come here."

"If you make me fly all the way to California, I'm not leaving without my daughter!"

This kind of hysterical declaration was, unfortunately, typical of his ex. "I have a custody order that says otherwise."

"I'll take her to Argentina if you force me."

That stopped him cold. A few minutes ago, he hadn't fully considered the implications of his ex's plan to leave the country. Had he foolishly agreed to send Fiona east with the nanny as requested, Sabrina might very well have fled with her, and now she'd raised the possibility of snatching his daughter from under his protection. "And you think threats will persuade me to trust you?"

Sabrina's tone changed to a cajoling whine. "Her birthday's next weekend. How can you separate a mother from her baby at a time like this? Remember how excited we were when we found out I was pregnant?"

Alec had been ecstatic, but worried, too, for his beautiful, fragile wife. When they'd first met, as graduate students at the University of Colorado's program in clinical science, he'd been dazzled by Sabrina. Tall and slim with dark hair, she'd shared his passion for biology and restored the sense of fun he'd missed since breaking up with Patty.

In retrospect, he wasn't sure how much of what he'd seen in Sabrina had been real and how much had been a projection of Patty's adventuresome nature. Still, they'd had fun together during their courtship, and for a brief time had settled happily into marriage. Then, gradually, Sabrina's behavior had become more erratic and self-centered.

After she gave birth to Fiona her mood swings intensified, as did her selfish demands for money and attention. Alec had arranged joint therapy sessions and sought the best medical care for what he'd believed were hormonal fluctuations. A psychiatrist had prescribed medication that took the edge off the mood swings but did nothing to stem what he'd finally realized was Sabrina's underlying narcissism.

For two years, Alec had felt as if he were parenting both his baby daughter and his wife, even as he earned his PhD then moved his family to Boston. By then, Sabrina had abandoned her career plans, which would have been fine if she'd taken good care of their daughter. Instead, one day that was etched forever into Alec's memory, he'd returned home unexpectedly and found her in bed with another man. In the nursery, Fiona was wailing to be fed.

He should have foreseen then how untrustworthy his wife was. He should have fought harder for custody right from the start....

"Alec?" Sabrina cooed, pulling him out of his reflections. "She can come visit me, can't she? I'll bet the nanny would enjoy a side trip to Boston to see her family. And my parents would love to spend some time with their granddaughter."

Her parents, who were highly educated but emotionally distant, also lived in New York. They'd stayed on civil terms with Alec and he knew for a fact that they rarely saw Sabrina.

"You can come here if you like," he repeated. "That's the only thing I'll allow."

"Oh?" With one sharp word, she returned to vixen mode. "You better keep a close eye on our little girl, Alec Denny, because she's likely to disappear when you least expect it." With that, she clicked off.

His numb fingers fumbled the phone as he put it away. While he didn't exactly believe Sabrina intended to kidnap Fiona and take her to Argentina, he couldn't dismiss the possibility, either.

Now what was he going to do?

PATTY WISHED SHE HAD a video of Glenn Jerome/Jergens pretending to be affable as he squirmed in his booth. While Judi chattered on, the man kept nodding and fingering the edge of his plastic-coated menu until it frayed.

From his body language, she gathered he was trying to talk the young woman into leaving with him. She appeared oblivious as she ordered food and accepted refill after refill of coffee.

Patty checked her watch. Nearly two-thirty. She hoped this pair would wrap it up soon.

What if Judi left with the guy? It seemed unlikely she'd be imprudent enough to get into a car with him, but you never could tell. Some people had a stunning lack of the self-preservation instinct. Also, Patty didn't trust her ability to follow them in traffic. In real life, tailing a target was a lot harder than it looked in the movies.

She dialed the Finnegans' number. As prearranged, Judi's parents had stationed themselves nearby and could arrive in a couple of minutes. Patty had already informed them and Mike of Glenn's license number and real name. "If she starts to walk out with him, would you rather I confronted them?"

"Either way, she'll realize we've been spying," the mother said.

"True. Wait. She's getting up…heading for the ladies' room." Must be all that coffee.

"What's he doing?"

Patty kept watch with her peripheral vision. "Sneaking a glance around. Taking something out of his pocket." A small vial. "He just dumped something in her cup!"

"That's it! We're on our way."

"And I'm calling the police." She clicked off and dialed 911. As soon as Patty sketched the circumstances, she could hear the dispatcher radioing a black-and-white.

A man didn't drop something into a woman's cup without gravely evil intentions. Patty had to make sure Judi didn't drink it. She also had to handle the situation with care—Glenn might very well be armed, and even if he wasn't, he could grab a knife off the table and take the girl or someone else hostage.

Too bad Patty was going to be late to the wedding. But she had more important matters to deal with.

HARD AS ALEC STRUGGLED not to make too much of his ex-wife's threat, it preyed on his mind. Not that there weren't distractions. Running Fiona downstairs to his mother's, he found Darlene furious that one of her housekeeper's nieces, filling in for the ailing woman, had whacked a shelf of souvenir mugs with the vacuum and shattered a couple of mementos from Mom and Dad's travels.

"How many nieces can one woman have?" Darlene fumed after informing him that she'd just fired the girl. "I wish Marla would either come back or quit so I could hire someone else."

"You could put Marla on notice. Show up regularly or get fired," Alec pointed out as he opened a chest of toys in his mother's den and helped Fiona pick out a coloring book. The unit was a smaller version of his, stuffed with possibly even more toys.

"I can't do that! She's been with me for years, and she does excellent work when she's here," Darlene said. "And she needs the job."

"Well, at some point we'll have to hire a permanent replacement." But Alec didn't press the point. Although Marla and her substitutes technically worked for him, too, he respected his mother's kind heart too much to insist.

His gaze fell on the sliding door, which she'd left open to the patio. Only a low wall and a couple of hanging plants divided it from the parking lot. *Someone could hop right over.*

"Why are you staring out there?" demanded his mother. "Did one of the fuchsias die?"

"I'm concerned about safety." Catching her frown, he explained in a low voice, "Sabrina's making noises about snatching Fiona."

"She wouldn't get far!" Darlene exclaimed. "You have custody."

"I'm not sure how much good that would do in Argentina,"

Alec replied. "She's moving there with her boyfriend. For a while, at least."

A ferocious glare transformed his birdlike mother into a hawk. "I'd tear her eyes out!"

"Mom!"

"Just let her try."

Torn between amusement and concern, Alec said, "Maybe we should report this to the police."

"Report what? That your ex is acting crazy again? I wish that was a crime, but I doubt it," his mother scoffed.

"Then let's consider hiring some security."

"We have an alarm system. Let's start using it," she countered.

"Alarms don't work unless you close the doors," he pointed out. "And she specifically mentioned Fiona's birthday." They'd scheduled a party for next Saturday at a kid-oriented pizza parlor, inviting some new friends from the neighborhood and children of Alec's coworkers.

"She wouldn't ruin her own daughter's birthday!" Darlene looked shocked.

"Oh, wouldn't she?"

Fiona returned with a juice bar she'd retrieved from Grandma's freezer. "What about my birthday?"

"We were just discussing our plans." After giving them each a hug, Alec went out, leaving the subject unfinished. It needed more thought, but not right now.

He had no idea where the time had gone, but he was running late. He called Bailey, who agreed to meet him at the wedding chapel. A good thing, because by the time he dressed and drove the short distance, it was a quarter to four.

Cars crammed the small lot wedged between bluff-topped buildings. Alec circled his large sport utility vehicle in search of a space, and found one half-hidden between the two structures. Unfortunately, the open rear door of an aging sedan blocked his access.

The person he glimpsed inside must be digging around to find a wedding present, judging by the odd scrambling motions. Well, no sense in both of them being late, Alec reflected, and tapped his horn to let the driver know he was waiting.

An arm shot out the door. The attached fist formed the universal signal for "get lost."

"Give me a break," Alec muttered irritably, and hit the horn again.

The fist vanished, but now the occupant kicked the door open even wider. Two sock-clad feet and a pair of loose-fitting black pants stuck out. Judging by the wiggling, the idiot was pulling on his pants. Changing clothes, right here in the parking lot.

Alec had no intention of abandoning the only available space. Leaving the SUV in the aisle, he marched over. "Hey! I need to park. How about a little consideration?"

Then he noticed that the black pants had a satin tuxedo stripe up the side. And that the person squirming around in the back seat wasn't a guy, but a woman with straight blonde hair and an aggrieved thrust to her jaw.

He nearly laughed out loud, except he doubted Patty would appreciate his amusement. Seeing her felt good, though. Damn, he'd missed her and her shenanigans.

Patty executed a quick movement that brought her face into scowling range. "How about you stick your space-hogging... Oh, hey, Alec."

"What's going on?" he asked, and gave up trying to stifle his grin.

"I'm the maid of honor," she said as if that explained everything. "Just finished a job."

"Why aren't you getting dressed in the bridal chamber?"

"Can you do that?" she asked as she fastened her pants. "I've never been in a wedding before."

"I believe they reserve a room for the bride and her attendants." Never mind—she was nearly dressed, anyway. Then he spotted a brownish-red patch on her cheekbone. "Where'd you get the bruise?"

"Creep tried to roofie my client's daughter right in the middle of a restaurant." As usual, she spoke in a kind of verbal shorthand.

"You got into a fight?" Alec couldn't think of any other woman who would take a punching match in stride. He didn't much like the idea that Patty put herself at risk as part of her job, but he admired her courage. Always had.

"Yeah." A couple of black slip-on shoes hit the pavement. Patty stuck her feet in them and stood up, tucking a white shirt into the pants. She didn't seem to notice how invitingly the shirt stretched over her full breasts. "You gonna help or what?"

"Oh. Sure." Since she obviously didn't need help tucking in her shirt, he peered at the heap of junk in the backseat, registering a badly folded newspaper, take-out bags, a baseball cap, a pair of jeans and a T-shirt, sneakers, a worn duffel bag and, perched on top, a shiny black jacket. Alec handed it to Patty.

"Thanks, but that's not the problem." She gestured down at the pants, which hung well over the shoes. "Can you believe this? They aren't hemmed!"

"You didn't try it on first?"

"I ordered it and it just arrived yesterday. I'm five-eight. Pants are never too long for me." She frowned. "I thought I had a stapler, but I can't find it. You got any tape?"

Staple the hem of her pants? He supposed the idea made sense in the spontaneous world of Patty Hartman. "I might. Hang on." From the SUV's map compartment, he retrieved a roll of double-sided tape. "Good thing I like to be prepared."

"You were always good with your hands." Patty gave him a meaningful look.

Heat shimmered through Alec at the memory of touching her, everywhere. Well, almost everywhere. They'd gone at each other with an intensity his post-adolescent self had outgrown. Or had never managed to find again, and somehow convinced himself he didn't need.

To cover his response, he knelt and set to performing an emergency operation on her hem. He did his best to ignore the debris from the pavement digging into his knees. "So this jerk decked you?"

"Kind of."

"Kind of? You've got the bruise to prove it." Alec heartily wished he could return the favor to whoever had targeted Patty.

"Looks can be deceiving. See, there was this girl meeting a scumbag she contacted on the internet. Even though he's obviously twice the age he said he was, she sits right down, and then leaves her coffee unprotected while she goes to the bathroom. Then he pours something in it."

Her body braced as if preparing to do battle all over again. One knee grazed Alec's temple, almost like a caress. "Stop fidgeting."

"I'm late! Just stick the hem so it doesn't drag on the ground."

"Yes, that would be the idea," he replied dryly. Easier said than done. The fabric had to be folded and smoothed so it didn't wrinkle, and his hands kept brushing her bare ankle. And itching to move upwards....

"So, she lifts this doctored coffee but doesn't drink. Instead, she stares at him and roars, 'How dare you prey on girls like me! What do you think we are, objects put here for your perverted pleasure?'"

"She set him up?"

"Yeah. Turns out she blogs about the perils of online dating and set out to find a fellow she could write about. How do you like that?"

"I'd say he deserved it." Alec set to work on the second pant leg.

Patty ruffled his hair lightly. "Great haircut. You get that around here? Some of the cops could use a good barber."

"No, in Boston. But you can do that again," he murmured, his scalp tingling.

"What?"

"You want to scratch me around the ears, too? I always liked that."

Patty chuckled. "Keep working down there, will you?"

"Nearly done." Alec tore off a last piece of tape. "You still haven't explained how you got the bruise."

"The guy was ticked," Patty said. "He lunged across the table and grabbed her neck. Obviously, I had to take him out."

"And he punched you in the cheek." Again, Alec felt the urge to hunt down the man and smack him one in return.

"Naw. Judi threw her coffee on him. Good aim, only her elbow caught me and wham! Lights, sound and music. Quite a show. It'll be a fun shade of purple by tomorrow."

He straightened and brushed off his knees. So it had been an accident. "Glad you're okay."

She glanced down at her newly hemmed pants. "Nice job."

"Tell me you had this guy arrested. I don't like to think about him running loose."

"Oh, the police got there a minute later and hauled him away in cuffs," Patty assured him. "The evidence in the coffee is kaput, but they found the vial in his pocket. They'll be testing that for residue."

A totally unrelated question came to Alec. "By the way, how come you're wearing a tux instead of a dress?"

"I hate dresses." She swung the car door shut.

"You looked beautiful at the homecoming dance." He'd been stunned at Patty's sensuality in a low-cut neckline and teasingly thigh-high skirt.

"And that worked out so well for me." She grabbed the rest of her gear and strode toward the chapel.

She'd given up wearing dresses because he'd broken up with her a few days later? It hadn't occurred to Alec until now how powerful an impact their breakup might have had on his sturdy girlfriend. She'd always seemed so resilient.

Yet twelve years later she refused to wear a bridesmaid's dress to her friends' wedding. He'd hurt her, and he regretted that, deeply.

Maybe he was taking too much blame for her wardrobe choices. In many ways, Patty was the strongest woman he'd ever met.

Then it came to him. Who better to supervise security for his daughter? Fiona already liked Patty, and his mother probably wouldn't mind having a woman guard around nearly as much as a male. And Alec couldn't think of anyone he'd rather spend time with than his old friend.

It was the best idea he'd had all day. Now all he had to do was persuade Patty to go along with it.

Chapter Five

Brides were always beautiful, but to Patty, Nora Kendall eclipsed them all. Blonde with green eyes, she could have passed for a stereotypical cheerleader—exactly Leo's type— except for that knowing spark in her gaze. Instead of white, she'd chosen a stunning dress of beige with rose-colored panels. It flattered her skin tone and disguised the slight swell that, six months from now, would produce a young Nora or Leo.

"Sorry I'm late," Patty said in the entry hall as she joined Nora and her father, Dwight Halvorsen, a tall, gray-haired man Patty had met the previous night at the rehearsal. The guests were already seated on the other side of a curtained doorway, except for Alec, who appeared a moment later looking apologetic as he slipped through a side entrance into the chapel.

"That's fine. I wasn't worried, since you called," Nora replied, with remarkable calm for a bride.

She hadn't acted flustered last night at the rehearsal, either, or the previous week at her bridal shower. That seemed odd to Patty, until Nora explained that she'd had a much grander wedding years ago. "I wasted a lot of energy on a guy who made a lousy husband. This time, I'm marrying the right man, and I intend to enjoy myself."

"I can vouch for Leo," Patty had said. "He's a great partner.

I mean, in the purely cop-type sense. But probably in the husband-type sense, too."

"Having you here means a lot to both of us."

"Me, too. Thanks for being a good sport." Patty knew Nora could have had her pick of bridesmaids, including Bailey, several girl cousins and her old friend and obstetrician, Paige Brennan. That had to be a first, the bride's obstetrician throwing her a shower. Patty had been kind of a klutz at most of the games, until it came to aiming pink beribboned darts at a heart-shaped board. She'd nailed that one, and taken home red-and-black thong panties as her prize. They might come in handy as a gag gift one of these days.

"Are you all right?" Dwight indicated her cheek. "That's a nasty contusion."

Contusion? Oh, yeah, he was a biology professor, Patty recalled. "I got a little too close to somebody's elbow. No big deal."

A pink-suited woman who worked for the wedding chapel materialized from a hallway. "Everybody ready?" she asked. "Maid of honor, where's your bouquet?"

Good question.

"You mean this isn't for me?" With a wink, Dwight Halvorsen handed Patty a mound of pink and purple flowers.

"Mmm." Patty buried her nose in them. "Smells great."

"It's four o'clock." For the first time, Nora sounded a little nervous. Well, naturally. This was a big moment.

From within the chapel, the buzz of voices sank to a murmur. The bearded young photographer who'd captured Patty's arrival disappeared into the interior.

"You remember what to do?" Nora asked.

"Uh, walk?"

"Slowly."

"Yeah. Right." The minister had joked about the fact that

there was no prize awaiting her at the altar. Not this time, anyway.

Patty had been certain she could tame her normally free-swinging stride. Now, she wasn't so sure. She could still feel the adrenaline pumping from her rush to get here, and from being close to Alec. Feeling his breath on her ankles, touching his thick hair… It wasn't fair that the old reactions kept sneaking back. Not fair at all.

From inside, piano music provided her cue. "Deep breath," the pink-suited woman told Patty, and counted out an agonizingly slow "One…two…three…" to set the pace. Then she pulled aside the velvet curtain.

"One…two…three…" Patty tried to keep the count, but she preferred to concentrate on the faces peering at her. She spotted Detective Captain Alan Reed, who was Leo's boss, and officers George Green and Bill Sanchez, who'd driven past her the other day. Kate Franco, Leo's sister-in-law. Bailey Wayne, Nora's nurse, who'd been a few years behind Patty in high school. They'd been friends, although they hadn't kept in touch.

Wait a minute. Why was Bailey sitting with Alec? They both worked at the medical center. Could they be, like, dating?

Why should you care, anyway?

She dragged her gaze to the row in front of them, where Mike's head and shoulders stuck up above the people around him—no surprise, since he was six foot four. He gave Patty a thumbs-up. Apparently he approved of the way she'd handled the restaurant ruckus.

At the altar, Leo waited beside his brother, Tony. A pair of handsome, brown-haired guys in tuxes, they stood braced the same way, with their feet slightly apart. Both very steady, the kind of men you could count on.

Patty inhaled as she reached them. She'd forgotten about counting. "Too fast?" she muttered to Leo.

"Can't be fast enough for me," he replied.

She took her position on the other side of the altar, abuzz with anticipation as the music changed to a wedding march. The curtain drew back again, and in stepped Nora on her father's arm.

The swell of music, the scent of flowers, the graceful approach of a woman so lovely that every bridal magazine in the world ought to feature her on the cover… How did that feel? Patty wondered. She couldn't picture herself in the role. She'd never dreamed about choosing a gown or picking bridal colors or seeing the man she loved standing by the altar, bursting with happiness.

If she'd toyed with the idea once or twice, back when she was dating Alec, Patty had long ago discarded those reflections. The few other lovers she'd had through the years hadn't even come close.

Besides, there'd been no room for frills or romanticism in her upbringing. The first home she remembered was a cluttered, hippie-style pad where her parents spent most of their sporadic earnings on marijuana. By the time they'd cleaned up their act, social workers had removed Patty and Drew to their grandfather's loving but stern home.

Now here she stood across from Leo, whose face glowed as he reached to take his bride from her father. Nora beamed up at him, her happiness a testament to second chances.

Was Patty getting tears in her eyes? How humiliating. Except, thank goodness, other people were crying, too. Until now, she'd never understood why people cried at weddings. It must be the memories.

With an effort, she managed not to look at Alec. Well, not straight at him. She could tell he didn't have his arm around Bailey or anything.

What was going on with them?

ALEC DIDN'T CARE MUCH for weddings. He supposed his antipathy dated from his own seven years earlier. Sabrina's parents had sprung for an elaborate affair, but insisted on holding it in Manhattan, even though the bride, groom and most of their friends lived in Colorado. There'd been a long weekend filled with dinners and parties, where he'd stood around in uncomfortable clothes greeting strangers—relatives and business acquaintances of his new in-laws—and watching his wife-to-be waver between euphoria and irritability.

He'd figured the moodiness would pass. He'd been wrong.

Now, while Bailey chatted with a couple of people from the hospital, Alec saw Patty posing for photos with the rest of the bridal party in one corner of the banquet hall. She'd made quite an impression striding up the aisle in her tuxedo, wearing her bruise like a badge of honor.

Patty the warrior. Patty the fierce protector. Exactly what his daughter needed.

As soon as the photographer released his subjects, Alec tapped Bailey's shoulder. "I know they don't plan a formal receiving line, but let's go congratulate the bride and groom."

"Great! And I'd love to talk to Patty. She was so nice to me in high school, even though I was an underclassman." Vivacious, with short, curly brown hair and a sprinkling of freckles, Bailey spilled out words as naturally as she breathed. "My family was a mess—my older sister, Phyllis, had to practically raise me. Patty understood, because she lived with her grandfather. She made me feel normal."

"Normal counts a lot when you're a teenager." Not that Alex had wasted his energy worrying about being popular. Getting high grades and test scores, taking advanced placement courses and being accepted by the right college had been his fixation. That, and spending as much time as possible with Patty.

His two passions had collided with a fury at the worst

possible moment. And he'd nearly made the wrong choice. Although he sometimes wondered about what might have been, he'd never doubted his decision.

As he guided Bailey toward the bridal couple, the crowd gathered around them. The knot of well-wishers was so thick, Alec and Bailey stopped short, their view half blocked by the towering man in front of them.

The throng parted as Patty came diving through. She accepted a chorus of greetings with a friendly "Back at ya!" and headed straight toward Alec. Good. He'd been hoping they could find a moment to talk.

Ignoring him, she addressed the giant. "So, Mike, you grab anything to eat yet?"

"Did you tell Leo I was here as your guest? He gave me a strange look," the man said. "I'm not one of his closest pals from the department, you'll recall."

"Might have slipped my mind."

The guy touched her cheek. "That's turning an interesting shade."

"Purple?"

"Among others."

"Good advertising," she announced.

Who was this Mike person? Alec wondered grumpily. If Patty meant anything to him, why didn't he protect her from flying elbows and drink-doctoring weirdos?

Alec was trying to figure out how to draw her attention when Bailey beat him to it by calling out, "Patty!"

She gave her a friendly wave. "Hey, Bailey."

"Guess what?" the nurse cried in a voice that carried over the hum of conversation. "I'm pregnant!"

Alec could have sworn every single person in the ballroom, right down to a waitress cleaning up a spilled drink, turned to look.

As for Patty, she wasn't smiling at Bailey. She was glaring straight at Alec.

PATTY'S RUSH OF OUTRAGE surprised her. Why should she be so upset that Alec Denny, barely arrived in town, had decided to make babies with an old friend from high school who wasn't her?

She'd just never imagined he felt that way about the bubbly underclassman. Patty was almost certain the two hadn't dated way back then. So how and when had they reconnected? And what was this business about having babies, anyway? Wasn't one daughter enough?

Mike was watching her curiously, so she dug deep and said, "Congratulations, Bailey. And you, too, Alec."

They both blinked as if she'd said the wrong thing. Patty was good at that, but this time she felt fairly certain she'd observed the social graces. In case she'd left anything out, however, she added, "I'm sure Fiona will love having a little brother or sister."

"Yes, that's wonderful news," added her companion, extending his hand. "Hi, I'm Mike Aaron. Patty works with me at Fact Hunter Investigations."

"Alec Denny. Director of the new laboratories at Safe Harbor Med Center." The men shook hands. "There seems to be a misunderstanding."

Yeah? This Patty had to hear.

"Oh, it's not *Alec's* baby." Bailey was practically hopping up and down with excitement. "I'm a surrogate for my sister and brother-in-law. Isn't that cool? I mean, I wish Alec could have helped, but he wasn't here."

Mike and Alec seemed at a loss for words. "Yeah, he's quite a stud," Patty said.

The nurse flushed as red as a valentine. "I mean, because he's a clinical embryologist. Instead, I went to this center in L.A."

"What exactly is a clinical embryologist?" Mike asked.

Alec responded with practiced professionalism. "I work

with human embryos. Once our labs are set up, we'll perform in vitro fertilization, process sperm for artificial insemination and handle a variety of related processes."

"You use sperm donors?" Mike inquired.

"That's part of it," Alec said. "We also help couples conceive their own genetic babies using less than optimal eggs or sperm, and in some cases we can prevent birth defects. The field is rapidly advancing and Safe Harbor will have the most up-to-date facilities available."

"About these donors. I've always wondered—where do you find them?" Mike asked.

Patty nearly teased him about wanting to become one, but decided against it. Mike's sense of humor could be unpredictable.

"Sperm banks advertise at universities and other likely places to find acceptable donors," Alec said. "Others put ads on the internet, but we have to be very careful." He explained that donors were screened for infectious and genetic diseases, personal histories, physical characteristics and personality traits.

Patty only half listened. She was still enjoying the fact that Alec wasn't about to become a father again and that Bailey, given her condition, wasn't likely to be in the market for a guy right now.

"You and Patty are both detectives?" Alec's question penetrated her thoughts.

"We are." Mike straightened, going on new-business alert. "I'm licensed by the state of California, and Patty works for me. Can we help you with something?"

"Possibly."

Mike handed him a card. "I have eleven years' experience as a police officer, including five years as a detective, plus a master's degree in criminal science."

"Do you handle security?" Alec asked.

What was going on? Patty wasn't sure she liked the idea of having Alec as a client. If she were assigned to guard him, she might have a little trouble keeping her mind on her work. Anyway, why would he need guarding?

Mike was forging ahead smoothly. "We're a small agency, but we are licensed to do bodyguard and security work. I can make a referral if you need crowd control."

"It's more in the nature of…" Alec glanced around. "We should talk privately."

"I'd be happy to meet with you later," Mike said.

"For this job, I'd need Patty."

What? She struggled to keep her tone level. "Detectives aren't supposed to get personally involved in cases." To Mike, she explained, "We used to date."

"Oh, I'm not the one who needs protecting," Alec assured her.

Then who? But this wasn't the time or place to go into details, she supposed.

"I'm confident we can work this out, Dr. Denny," Mike assured him. "Give me a call and we'll set up an appointment. The three of us."

Alec tucked the card in his pocket. "I'd be glad to. But I have a PhD, not an MD. Whenever someone calls me doctor, I'm always afraid they're going to keel over and expect me to save their life."

"Patty and I are both trained in CPR. We'll handle the lifesaving part," Mike replied drily.

Patty wished she knew more about what was going on. Why would Alec be hiring a guard for someone else? If there was a threat against the lab, surely the hospital would call on its own security staff.

All the same, she was glad for an excuse to see him again, in a professional setting. In this small town, they could hardly avoid running into each other, and she'd like to reestablish their relationship on a platonic basic. That way, maybe she'd stop fantasizing about ruffling his hair and slipping her arms around his chest. And tilting her mouth up to his, and… *Now cut that out!*

People were beginning to line up at the buffet. The delicious scents of roast beef and salmon wafted over, reminding Patty that she'd missed lunch.

"If we're done here, I'll catch you later," she told Alec and Bailey.

"It's great to see you again." The nurse gave Patty a hug. "I hope Nora won't mind me breaking the news about my pregnancy at her wedding. I'm not trying to be the center of attention. She already knows, and when I saw you, I just had to tell you."

"I'm sure Nora won't mind." In Patty's opinion, the bride's state of euphoria should obliterate any such petty concerns.

She and Mike joined the line. "Good work," he murmured. "You brought in a client."

"He's my old boyfriend," Patty retorted. "You can't expect me to guard his body. Or…whoever."

"If he likes our work, the whole medical center will hear about it." Mike stepped aside to let a guest with a plate of food pass through the line. His path brought him into a collision course with a tall, red-haired woman Patty recognized from the bridal shower. "Sorry," he murmured.

"No problem." Despite the polite words, she sounded irritated.

As she moved away, Mike turned to Patty. "Who's the Amazon?"

The redhead swung toward him with a fierce expression. "That's a rude way to refer to me."

"My apologies," Mike said swiftly. "Actually, I like tall women."

Her lips tightened and she marched off without another

word. He ducked his head and waited a moment before asking, "Is she gone?"

"Disappearing into the crowd," Patty confirmed.

"Okay, now, who's the ticked-off Amazon?"

"That's Paige Brennan, the bride's obstetrician," Patty said. If Mike had any interest in the lady doc, he'd apparently blown his chances, but that wasn't her concern. "Do you suppose it's okay to take both the roast beef and the salmon?"

"You're the maid of honor. You can do anything you like."

"Yeah," she replied happily. "That's right. We're sitting at the head table, too. Does that mean we get extra champagne?"

"It means you have to make a toast," Mike said.

Uh-oh. "I do?" She wished she'd had some warning. What on earth would she to say?

"I'll give you a pointer," her boss offered. "No jokes about the wedding night."

"They already had the wedding night. Hence, the obstetrician," she pointed out, and moved forward to grab a plate.

Wedding nights. What an archaic custom, Patty thought, except for very religious people. Or shy ones. Or couples who'd never made it beyond heavy groping in the backseat of a car....

She'd better quit thinking that way, and fast. Or else figure out how to explain to Mike why she turned down whatever work Alec intended to offer.

Chapter Six

He should have talked to Patty before mentioning the job to her boss, Alec mused as he watched her joking with the other people at the head table. He hadn't meant to put her in an awkward position.

On the other hand, she might have refused, and then where would he be? All things considered, Alec was glad for Mike Aaron's obvious interest in landing a new client.

Patty certainly had changed in the past decade. She moved with more confidence, and despite her less-than-feminine attire, she exuded a natural sexuality. He tried not to think about watching her get dressed out in the parking lot, the way her blouse had emphasized her full breasts, the way he'd felt an intense longing to get closer to this new, more sophisticated Patty.

In the old days, they'd fooled around plenty. He'd made it to first base and beyond, but never... Now why was a mature, divorced man with a four-year-old child using high-school terms like "first base"? Or even considering undressing a woman who might be working for him?

Patty had a point. If he intended to hire her to run security, he couldn't allow either of them to get distracted.

As he sat at a table with a group of fellow hospital staff, Alec replayed his earlier conversation with his ex-wife.

The threat had felt serious at the time, but perhaps he was overreacting.

"You better keep a close eye on our little girl, Alec Denny, because she's likely to disappear when you least expect it." No, he wasn't letting his fears get the best of him. That had been a direct threat.

"I'll take her to Argentina if you force me." With that declaration, she'd upped the stakes, because she could take advantage of a possible conflict in international child custody laws. If Sabrina married this boyfriend and stayed in Argentina, a court there might claim jurisdiction.

The expense would be staggering, and months or years might pass while he fought to get his daughter back. It was unimaginable to be separated from Fiona. Worse, he had no faith in Sabrina's ability to provide a safe, loving home.

Alec tensed, the adrenaline surging. Maybe he should leave now, drive home and check on Fiona. Or at least call his mother to be sure nothing had gone wrong.

Oh, for Pete's sake, you talked to Sabrina only a few hours ago. She hadn't had time to put a plan in motion, assuming that she ever would.

How ironic that Alec spent his life helping other couples have children, and now he risked losing his own. But how many people, when they married, thought about what kind of parent their partner would make? Or how they might act in a custody battle? Even if anyone tried to warn him about Sabrina, he doubted he'd have listened.

"I wish I could have the baby at Safe Harbor, but my sister insists on me using a doctor in L.A.," Bailey was telling their tablemates. "She's going to be my birthing coach, so that should be fun."

"What about your brother-in-law?" Mark Rayburn asked. "Surely he'll be involved in the pregnancy, too."

"Boone's a funny guy." It was the first note of uncertainty

Alec had heard from the nurse. "He doesn't show much excitement, considering how lucky he is to be having a baby that's genetically his own. It's probably because they've had a few ups and downs recently with their investment company. Men tend to have one-track minds, don't they?"

"I'm sure he'll warm up," said pediatrician Samantha Forrest, who was married to Mark. "How are you feeling? Carrying a baby for another woman must be quite a challenge."

Bailey patted her abdomen. "I'm glad I can repay Phyllis for all she's done. She's twelve years older than me and acted more like a mother than our real mom. Plus, she and Boone have already doubled my savings through investments. I should be able to start my courses to become a nurse practitioner as soon as I recover from the birth."

"Good for you!" Mark broke off as, at the head table, someone rang a bell for attention.

The best man stood and raised his glass. "I'd like to say a few words about my brother."

The groom stared at the ceiling. "Uh-oh. Here we go."

"I promise not to mention what a holy terror you were as a child."

"You just did."

"Oops."

Alec grinned. He didn't know these men very well, but there was something endearing about their obvious rapport.

"All joking aside, it's hard to believe that only three months ago, Leo was best man at *my* wedding." Tony, who as hospital attorney had been helping Alec review construction contracts, beamed at the pretty woman sitting beside him. "My wife and I never expected to have another wedding in the family so soon, or to be welcoming a nephew."

When he paused, a ripple ran through the room. "Are you telling us it's a boy?" Samantha called.

"Oh, did I let something slip?" Tony teased.

Cheers rang out. The bride and groom, who'd obviously authorized this leak, smiled at each other and clasped hands on the table.

"I understand they're planning to name him Socrates, is that right?" the best man went on.

"Einstein," Leo corrected, while Nora poked him in the side.

Alec chuckled. How easily and naturally this family interacted. He tried to remember the toasts at his own wedding, but they'd long since faded. His best man had been a fellow PhD candidate with whom he hadn't spoken since graduation.

"To a wonderful couple that I'm proud to call my family. To Leo and Nora!" Tony took a swallow of champagne, and everyone else followed suit, although it appeared Nora was drinking water, as was Bailey.

At the head table, Mike gave Patty a meaningful look. Alec could have sworn she mouthed the words, *Do I have to?* At his nod, she got to her feet and raised her glass. The room fell silent again.

"I better warn you guys that there are police officers present, including the groom, so if you've had more than a few glasses of this stuff, you better sleep it off before driving home," she announced, and pretended to sit down. "Oh, I'm not finished?" She straightened. "Sorry about that."

"Give 'em heck, Patty!" called a fellow with short hair and a trim mustache. Most likely one of the officers, Alec mused, and wondered what it had been like for Patty, serving with a bunch of macho men. She'd always liked guy stuff, so she'd probably loved every minute of it.

"The first time I met Nora, I pegged her the wrong way because she's a lot prettier and blonder than I am," Patty said. "And Leo had a bad track record with the ladies…. Oh, I'm not supposed to mention that. Well, she set me straight in the nicest way. I wish I could figure out how she does that. My goal in life is to be as a gracious as Nora, but still whip Leo's butt at pool. Which I can do with one hand tied behind my back—if anybody's interested, I'm giving two-to-one odds for the next match. I'm renting his old house with the pool table."

"I'm in!" yelled the mustachioed guest, waving a five-dollar bill.

"Yo, George, don't think you can back out of it, either," Patty said.

Leo laughed and slipped an arm around his wife's waist. "I look forward to teaching you a lesson. Again."

"Here's to the best partner a former cop ever had, and to his wonderful new partner in life. To Nora and Leo!" Patty declared.

There were cheers and champagne all around. Conversations hummed pleasantly. Alec was glad he'd come, and not only for professional reasons. He genuinely liked his new coworkers and their friends.

All the same, as Nora made the first cut in the cake, Alec hoped the reception would wind up quickly. He'd like to discuss the security issue with Patty privately.

While the caterer took over the task of cutting and plating the cake, a deejay invited everyone onto the dance floor. Alec asked Bailey to join him, and soon they were gyrating in a crowd of merrymakers.

Glancing over, he noted that Patty's style of dancing involved bumping hips with her partner—Mike apparently didn't dance, so she'd chosen George—while occasionally pumping her fists and shouting with glee. The energy level in the room swelled, and if her earlier dustup had left any soreness, she gave no sign.

"She was always such a whirlwind," Bailey said when she and Alec retreated to their table, leaving Patty tearing up the floor with another fellow. "In high school, even the snobby girls were in awe. She wasn't afraid of anyone or anything."

"I doubt she worried about the snobby girls," Alec mused. "She made up her own rules. It was great."

"I felt like this complete dorky outsider until I met her. After that, I was still dorky, but not such an outsider." With scarcely a pause, Bailey added, "Why'd you two break up?"

She asked the question so artlessly that Alec responded without thinking. "She brought out my rebellious side and it scared me. I'm not sure if I was trying to sabotage myself, but I got drunk the night before the SATs. It wasn't her fault, it was mine. I realized I had to break it off because as long as I hung around her, I wasn't sure what I might do next. I wanted my career, yet I had this crazy streak, too."

"You broke up with her because you messed up one time?" Bailey demanded skeptically.

"There were other scrapes, too." While he recalled them fondly, Alec had to admit he'd taken inexcusable risks. "One night we went skateboarding on campus, which was against the rules. The next day, we found out some other kids had spray-painted the gym that night and broken a couple of windows. If anyone had seen us, we might have taken the blame and been expelled. At the moment, we were just glad for our narrow escape, but later I saw how close I'd come to throwing away my future."

The nurse sipped a cup of decaf. Around them, the table was empty, but a scattering of purses indicated their seatmates planned to return. "Patty said your parents made you drop her."

"My first SAT scores were well below where they needed to be. My folks said if I didn't land a scholarship, I'd have to borrow the difference between the total cost and what they'd saved for me. That would have meant tens of thousands of dollars in loans." That conversation had been Alec's first encounter with hard financial reality. He'd also had to confront the possibility that, if he didn't bring up his scores, he might not be accepted to his first choice college.

"So your parents didn't force you to break up?"

"I exaggerated," he admitted. "I told her they refused to pay any of my tuition if I kept seeing her. I should have told the truth, that it was my decision, but I was too immature. Besides, I liked her so much, I was afraid I'd cave in and change my mind."

"You guys seemed so grown-up, being two years older than me," Bailey said. "It's hard to remember that you were only seventeen."

"I'd always been such a well-behaved, obedient kid, and being around Patty brought me this rush of freedom. Breaking the rules was exciting. I had to outgrow that stage, and I couldn't do it with her." He still felt guilty about lying, but he didn't see the point of coming clean now. "You won't tell her, will you?"

"Of course not. That's between you and her." Kicking off her shoes, Bailey stretched her stockinged feet on a chair. "Feel free to go dance with someone else. I'm exhausted."

Dance with someone else. Who else but…?

On the floor, guests had formed a circle around Patty and her latest partner. To a hard-driving beat, she was dancing with boundless energy, laughing and making cracks that set her audience to chuckling. What if Alec dived in there, tapped the other guy and took his place? What fun to cut loose and howl the way they used to.

In front of all these new colleagues, including the hospital administrator? *I haven't changed as much as I thought.*

Alec could hardly expect them to take him seriously as a perfectionist in his labs and with his staff if they had an image stuck in their minds of him jumping around and screaming like a madman. Perhaps he was exaggerating the risk to his reputation, but then, he also represented Dr. Tartikoff.

It would have been fun, though.

The music ended amid a smattering of applause. "Well, folks, I'd love to stay, but I have it on good authority that the bride and groom are about to depart," announced the deejay. "For all you singles, there'll be the ritual tossing of the bouquet to determine who gets married next, so hurry out to the front steps to try your luck."

Bailey grabbed her purse. "Might as well give it a shot. Not that I'm even remotely looking for love right now, but you never know. Come on, Alec, you're single, too."

"And happy to stay that way." He could hardly refuse to accompany his date, though, so he went with her.

Outside, where a number of guests had assembled to observe, Alec descended the steps and took a position to one side, well out of danger of catching anything beyond a few dubious glances. Then Patty came out beside Mike.

"Feel free," she told her boss. "I am *not* doing this."

"You're the maid of honor. It's legally required," he replied.

With a grumble and a scowl, she took up a post on the opposite side of the steps from Alec, nearly out of flower-grabbing range.

Bailey didn't appear to have much of a chance, pitted against several tall women, including an obstetrician whom Alec had heard might be moving her practice to Safe Harbor to work with Dr. Tartikoff. Still, the nurse grinned at him gaily.

Cheers and applause erupted when the bride emerged into the fading daylight. "Everybody ready?"

"Ready as we'll ever be!" Bailey shouted.

The bride faced away from the guests and launched the mass of pink, purple and silver backward into the air. To Alec, it seemed to hang for a moment before choosing a trajectory straight toward Patty.

She gaped at it, laced her fingers together and swung, whacking it neatly into Bailey's waiting arms. Joking cries of "No fair!" and "What're you afraid of, Patty?" filled the air.

Nora whirled. "What happened?"

"Your maid of honor used it for batting practice," Leo said from his position next to his bride.

Bailey waved the trophy aloft. "I caught it!"

"And welcome to it." Patty dusted off her hands.

Amid smiles and congratulations to the bridal couple and the bouquet-winning nurse, the guests dispersed. Alec walked Bailey to her car. "I'll follow you home to make sure you arrive safely."

"Heck, no! Now that I have the bouquet, I might meet my true love any minute. Maybe some handsome officer will give me a ticket," she teased. "If it works, I'll lend it to you next."

"If it works, you should preserve it," he countered. "Thanks for bringing me."

"My pleasure."

When he reached his SUV, Alec saw Patty's car still in place. He supposed he ought to get behind the wheel and drive off, but after watching her buoyant spirits at the party, he missed his old friend. Until now, he hadn't realized exactly how much joy had gone out of his life on that long-ago day when he'd said goodbye to Patty and to part of himself.

Besides, he'd resolved to talk to her about Fiona. So, focusing on his perfectly good reasons for sticking around, he leaned against the car and waited.

Chapter Seven

Patty should have known she'd take her share of ribbing over the knocking-away-the-bouquet incident, but she hadn't expected everybody and his brother to get in on the action.

Mike said, "You could have hit it a little harder. I think there were a few petals still attached."

Bill Sanchez said, "You know, some girls like flowers." Then, eyeing her tux, he added, "Did anyone ever mention that you *are* a girl?"

Captain Reed dodged past her on the steps, playfully putting up his hands as if expecting her to give him a whack, too.

Leo said, "Getting married is great once you find the right person. Really, Patty." Of course, he could be excused for sappy sentimentality, seeing as it was his wedding day.

Patty was glad most of them didn't know her history with Alec, because if anyone had brought *that* up, no telling what she might have done.

Besides, no matter how cute he was, she'd come to terms with their breakup. His parents had lowered the boom, and he'd caved in. Maybe, as her grandfather had said, that made him unworthy of her, but she understood how important his education was.

Since then, they'd both moved on. She had only one major regret.

She wished they'd gone to bed together.

Not that she was sex-starved. A woman had no lack of opportunities in that department, especially when she worked in a macho environment as Patty had for years. But while she'd had a few affairs, the sex had always fallen short of spectacular.

Since Patty didn't believe the entire world was lying to her about the joys of sex, she assumed that either she lacked a certain key trait, kind of like being color-blind, or she hadn't done it with the right guy. At this point, she was well past wanting to do it with Alec, in theory at least, but she couldn't help wishing they'd tried. Because if any man was likely to light her fire, it would have been him.

Then at least she'd know what she was missing, or that she had some defect and wasn't missing anything. Without the fireworks, she didn't see much point in catching bouquets or putting on girlie clothes. Or in wearing some guy's ring and listening to him complain about her weird work hours and slugfests with felons.

Finally, the bride and groom descended the steps in a shower of birdseed—Californians were nothing if not environmentally correct—and rode off in a limo covered in flowers. Patty was free to enjoy the rest of her weekend. Breaking into her natural long stride, she cut across the parking lot and around the corner.

There he stood. Alec Denny. Alone. Watching her with a half smile that riveted Patty's attention on his mouth.

If he was such a great kisser, didn't it logically follow that he'd also be great at other things? With him divorced and her single, was it really out of the question…?

Yes.

"Thanks, but I don't need help changing." She unlocked her car. "I'll wear my tux home."

A glimpse of white teeth and the cleft in his cheek did

funny things to her nervous system. Until the last few days, Patty had almost forgotten she *had* a nervous system.

"I hope I didn't put you in an awkward position with your boss." Alec's velvety voice made it hard to concentrate on his words.

Oh, yeah, the security gig. "Why do you need me? Mike's got more experience."

"My daughter likes you."

She'd been kind of hoping *Alec* liked her, she realized to her embarrassment. Then the fact registered that this security business concerned Fiona. "Is she in some kind of danger?" Patty hated to think of anyone hurting a kid, and for some reason she felt an unusually powerful surge of protectiveness toward this one.

"Possibly. It concerns my ex-wife." Despite the sunlight, his brown eyes darkened.

"Custody issues? They can get touchy." Patty had once taken down an estranged husband the size of a sumo wrestler when he'd tried to snatch his kids in violation of a judge's order. She wouldn't care to try that again; her shoulders and arms had ached for days. Lucky thing Alec hadn't married a sumo wrestler.

"A judge granted me full custody after Sabrina left her alone in a car for over an hour." He swallowed hard at the memory.

Every year, several dozen children across the country died from heat exhaustion after being left in vehicles, sometimes for less than an hour. Under California law, it was a crime to leave a child under six alone in a vehicle under unsafe conditions, which, in Patty's opinion, meant any time longer than it took to run into a house and grab a forgotten lunch box. "What's wrong with her?"

"Sabrina's always been high-strung, but over the years she became increasingly self-centered and unstable."

That fit with what Fiona had said, or rather, with what she'd quoted her grandmother as saying. Patty hadn't been sure whether to trust the elder Mrs. Denny's assessment, until now. "I'd call that criminally negligent."

Alec blew out a long breath. "I felt responsible, even though it was a judge's decision to give her temporary custody. I should have fought harder. By some miracle, Fiona apparently slept through the whole thing, and the car was parked in an underground lot so it didn't heat up, but we were just lucky. The problem is, when Sabrina wants something, nothing else seems to matter."

Hence the current interest in security, apparently. "What's she up to now?"

"She threatened to snatch our daughter. At this point, I don't know how seriously to take it, but you can see why I'm concerned."

"Have you filed a report with the police? You should. For future reference if nothing else." The police might not be able to take immediate action, but that would put them on the alert in case of further developments.

"Fine. But I need more than that."

"Then Mike's the right guy for the job."

"And you're the right woman." Alec caught her hands. Instinctively, Patty noted the strength in his grip, despite his gentleness. Those were skilled hands, precise and controlled as they massaged hers gently. One of her former boyfriends had given her a whole body massage that hadn't made her as tingly as this did. "Sabrina threatened to take her out of the country. She's engaged to a guy from Argentina."

That raised the stakes. Reluctantly, Patty extricated her hands so she could think straight. "If she mentioned taking Fiona out of the country, that's more than a vague threat."

"How about if we continue this discussion at my place?" Alec asked. "The nanny went shopping and Fiona is at her grandmother's. You could take a look around to prepare your security recommendations."

And we'd be alone.

Oh, come on, Patty chided herself. She'd never backed away from a difficult situation, and maintaining her professional distance around Alec was nothing if not a challenge. "Where do you live?"

He ran a hand through his enticingly soft hair. "The Harbor Bluff Condo Development. It's a mile or so from here."

"That's where our bride and groom live." After Leo moved into Nora's first-floor unit, they'd invited Patty to a small dinner party. Swank place, great view.

"That's right. I've seen them around. So you'll come?"

As Patty had pointed out to Mike, a detective shouldn't get personally involved in a case. And being near Alec made her want to brush a stray leaf off his coat, and maybe kiss that wry smile off his mouth. All the more reason to prove to herself that she could handle him just fine.

"I'll make a quick assessment of the premises. But you'll have to wait for my recommendations until we meet with Mike."

"I'll set up an appointment for Monday," Alec promised. "If we can get started now, though, I'll feel better."

"Meet you there."

"Hold on. You'll need this." From his car, he produced a parking pass. "Put this on your windshield so you don't get towed."

As he handed Patty the plastic card, the sea breeze enveloped her in his subtle cologne, and she noticed a pulse in his throat, right below the curve of his jaw. She used to enjoy nuzzling him there, especially late in the day when he got a little sandpapery.

Patty stepped back. "Thanks."

He stood there breathing hard, and she wondered what he

was thinking. But all he did was nod in acknowledgment and get in his car.

After starting her engine, Patty called Mike and advised him of her plans. "I'll take lots of notes."

"It concerns his daughter? No wonder he wants a woman involved," Mike said. "Still, I can tell he's attracted to you. Make sure he keeps it strictly on the up-and-up."

"No problem," Patty said.

He grunted. "I don't suppose we should charge for a preliminary consult like this."

"Wouldn't feel right," she agreed.

"Okay. Let me know if he needs us to start before Monday."

"Will do."

A few minutes later, Patty turned onto Viewpoint Lane and, approaching the condos, began her analysis. The development had limited access in the back, she noted, with bluffs that would be hard to scale. High cement-block walls on either side were also likely to discourage the sort of woman who fussed over her clothes, although Patty didn't dismiss the possibility of Sabrina hiring someone to do her dirty work.

Would she really put her daughter at risk in a stranger's hands? There was no telling. People did stupid and illogical things.

In the front, a black wrought-iron fence separated the building from the sidewalk. A visitor parking lot, where Patty found a space, was prominently posted with signs about visitors requiring a permit and warning that trespassers would be towed. A remotely operated gate protected the residents' lot.

Although the condo building was two stories high, each unit appeared to be confined to a single level. The second floor units were accessed from an open portico.

There was no guard. In fact, when Patty got out, she discovered that there was no lock on the gate between the visitor parking and the walkway in front of the building.

Alec emerged from the private lot, striding toward her. "What do you think so far?"

"Any chance of getting a lock on the front gate?" she asked.

He shook his head. "Mom says there used to be one and residents were always locking themselves out and complaining about missed deliveries. A lot of the time people left it propped open."

Patty decided not to press to have one installed. As he'd pointed out, locks were easily circumvented. Anyone determined to enter could simply wait until a resident came along, make up an excuse and slip inside.

"False sense of security, anyway," she muttered, and followed him to a recess that held the outdoor staircase. "Elevator?"

He indicated one half-hidden in a corner, illuminated by a single light. Patty didn't like the layout of the stairs or the elevator. Despite the presence of a security camera, it would be easy for someone to hide and ambush the nanny or Alec's mother, or Alec, for that matter. In her notebook, she sketched a diagram of the area.

"That's Mom's unit." Stepping back from the alcove, Alec pointed to a first-floor condo. "Mine's above it and over one."

"Does Fiona spend much time in the lower unit?"

He nodded. Another weak point, Patty observed. "How much do you know about this nanny? Who hired her?" If it had been the ex-wife, the woman's loyalties could be in question.

"I did, after the split. One of my coworkers recommended her. They loved her, but their kids were getting too old for a nanny. And for the record, she and Sabrina can't stand each other."

"Could be an act."

"You don't know Tatum."

Satisfied for the moment, Patty continued asking about the child's schedule as they reached the second floor, and learned that Fiona hadn't yet enrolled in a nursery school since moving to California. Instead, the nanny and Grandma read to her and taught her about numbers, colors, shapes and letters during outings and play sessions.

Talking about his daughter brought a melting warmth to Alec's face. "She's so smart. Way ahead of most children her age—but what parent doesn't say that?" He shrugged helplessly. "I don't care if she's brilliant or ordinary by anybody else's standards. She's sweet and funny, and she depends on me utterly. If I ever fail her again…" Averting his face, he unlocked his door. A dead bolt, Patty noted approvingly.

Fatherhood suited Alec, she reflected, feeling a tug deep inside at this evidence of what a caring man he'd become. Maybe it was a good thing they'd split up, because she doubted she had much aptitude for family life, given what lousy role models her parents were. As for her grandpa, his method of child rearing had been to let her make her own choices until, with a few sharp words or a harsh look, he let her know that she'd failed him. Patty wouldn't care to inflict that approach on a child.

Alec's condo had a floor plan similar to Nora's, Patty soon discovered, with a large living room that opened into the den and a kitchen-dining area. The balcony was high enough above the carport below to pose a challenge to a would-be intruder, but that depended on how much risk someone was willing to run. Because of the staggered architectural design, the neighboring balconies weren't within easy climbing reach, but again, you never could tell. The heavy sliding glass door fastened securely.

Patty studied the main room, its walls and trim painted in shades of blue and gray. Unless you counted the fireplace or the skylight, both unlikely entry points, the only access was from the balcony, a couple of windows high enough not to be easily breached and the front door.

That was how intruders usually got into places like this. Someone inside simply opened the door, or left it unlocked.

The place had an alarm system, but it wasn't on when they arrived. "Ever change the security code in this thing?" she asked.

Alec shook his head. "My mom owns the place. She used to rent it out. Actually, she still does—to me."

"Change it." Patty jotted a reminder in her notebook, then cast a dubious glance at the delicate, cream-hued furniture. A few picture books and a red-and-white fleece blanket provided the only splashes of color. She felt a twinge of sympathy for Fiona, who probably had to be extra careful to keep her shoes off the couch. "Not exactly kid friendly."

"This was Sabrina's furniture." Alec ran his hand over a sculpted arm on the sofa. "She insisted on buying it when she was pregnant, then didn't want it in the divorce because it was damaged." He indicated a nick in the wood and a small stain on one cushion, which to Patty seemed merely evidence that a child lived here.

"How'd you ever marry this loser, anyway?" Immediately, she regretted the question. "Sorry. That was inappropriate."

He didn't seem perturbed. "Believe it or not, we had a lot of fun in the beginning."

Enough to produce a child, obviously. "Was she ever violent?"

He frowned. "What do you mean?"

"Did she ever lose her temper and throw things at you? Threaten you with a knife? Slap Fiona?"

His face registered shock. "Nothing like that."

"Any reason to think she might turn violent now?" Custody cases could bring out the worst in people.

He thought for a moment. "I've never considered Sabrina physically dangerous, but she's impulsive and she can get hysterical. I suppose she could overreact."

Patty was glad he didn't dismiss the idea out of hand. "What about this boyfriend?"

"I've never met him." Alec moved past her to the kitchen. "Care for anything to drink?"

She'd love a beer and popcorn, and to stretch out on the sofa next to Alec and watch whatever was on TV while they added a few more smudges to the upholstery. But this wasn't a social visit. "No, thanks. Got a picture of the ex?"

"In Fiona's room." He checked his watch. "I can't believe it's after seven already."

"What time are your people due back?" She'd like to meet this nanny, to assess her physical strength and also to get a sense of whether she might be vulnerable to bribery.

And to see if she's in love with her boss, which wouldn't be at all surprising. But then, the woman might be older. Like, fifty or sixty.

"I told them I'd be home by eight. They'll probably be arriving around then, also."

"We'd better finish up." Without waiting for an invitation, Patty walked into the bedroom wing. Just like at Nora's, there were three chambers. At one end of the hall, she peered into what must be the nanny's room, judging by the orderly arrangement of brushes and cosmetics on the bureau. Also, there was a large photo of three similar-looking, pretty young women. "Are those her daughters?"

Alec glanced at the picture. "No, that's Tatum in the middle, with her sisters."

Patty studied the lovely young woman with braided chestnut hair. So this was the nanny who worked and lived with Alec. But there'd been no hint of romantic interest in his manner when he spoke of her.

The room had only a small skylight. Fiona's bedroom, she soon discovered, came with a partly open window. The neighbor's balcony lay just far enough away to make access difficult but not impossible.

"Switch their rooms," Patty said.

"I'm sorry?"

"Someone could get in the window." She stopped. "I wasn't going to make recommendations today. But it's pretty obvious."

Alec leaned in the doorway. "Not that I doubted you, but I keep forgetting that you really do know your stuff. It's hard to picture you in a police uniform with a gun on your hip. Do you carry one now?"

She hadn't applied for a permit. "No. Mike does, but I'd rather avoid that kind of situation."

"You used to enjoy target practice when we were in high school."

"Sure." After they'd broken up, she'd gone out and shot a bunch of clay pigeons, picturing each of them as his head. "That was one of my best subjects at the police academy."

"Is that where you learned how to be a cop?"

"Partly. I also studied criminal justice in college. Later, I did some work toward a master's but dropped out when my grandfather died." With her brother in the army, she'd taken responsibility for sorting through Grandpa's possessions and selling his house, dividing the money equally among her, Drew and Rainbow. "I worked for the probation department for a few years before I got hired by the Safe Harbor P.D. They sent me to the police academy."

"What do they teach you there?"

"Crime-scene investigation. High-speed driving in a chase. Interview techniques. What evidence is admissible in court. Lots of stuff." Returning her attention to Fiona's room, Patty noticed a stuffed rabbit with a Band-Aid around one raggedy ear. "Your daughter shares your interest in medicine."

"She's a great kid. I hope she'll be her own person." He chuckled. "The truth is, I hope she'll get a great education and pursue her interests seriously, whatever they turn out to be."

"Hey, I can't blame you for wanting your daughter to have a purpose in life." Patty picked up a framed photo of a strikingly beautiful woman. Dark hair tumbled around an oval face with large brown eyes and a full mouth. "This would be the ex-wife?"

"That's Sabrina."

Patty didn't want to compare herself to this stunning creature, but she couldn't help it. "Guys must fall all over her."

"She's used to getting what she wants." He frowned.

Patty set the picture down and handed him a copy of her business card. "We'll need a JPEG of this and any other photos you have of her so we know who we're watching for. Can you email these to me?"

"Of course."

He stepped aside to let her exit. In the tight space, her hand brushed the smooth fabric of his suit jacket. Patty's reaction annoyed her. She had to stop feeling so keenly aware of Alec as a desirable man. If she didn't get over this, she'd never be able to do her job.

The moment she entered Alec's bedroom, she wished she could skip this part of the visit. He must have shared that bed with Sabrina, although the colorful quilt tossed over it looked new. In fact, the whole place was infused with Alec, from the masculine desk in one corner to the walk-in closet filled with neatly pressed suits, slacks and shirts.

Think about the job. She focused on diagramming, tracking the windows and yet another skylight. "Done here," she announced as quickly as she could.

"Patty." He stood in the doorway.

"Yeah?" She kept her face partly turned away, her hair screening her features.

"I didn't expect things to be so tense between us." Alec's voice rasped with uncharacteristic rawness.

"Tense?" she repeated. *Didn't do as good a job of hiding it as I thought.*

He moved closer, his broad shoulders obliterating everything else, his thumb tipping up her chin. "This shouldn't feel uncomfortable. We can still be friends."

She'd never been good at lying. "Like I told you, I'm the wrong person for the job."

"No. You're the right everything." As if he couldn't contain himself any longer, he lowered his head until his mouth met hers.

Slipping her arms around him, Patty tried to remember why she'd been so determined to keep her distance. And failed completely.

Chapter Eight

The heat of Alec's tongue, the softness of his hair beneath her palm, the hardness of his body against hers... Patty had forgotten how a kiss could rewire her entire system.

As Alec gathered her close, her hands moved instinctively up his chest. She wanted to touch him everywhere, to strip off these annoying clothes, to brush her bare skin against his. In response, he stroked beneath her tuxedo jacket, and her breasts burst with sensation against his palms.

The bed was so close. She had no doubt that, with Alec, sex would be all the things she'd heard about, read about, dreamed about....

With a groan of self-reproach, Patty stepped back. Held him at bay until her gaze cleared, and they stood staring at each other.

"I didn't mean to—" He broke off, breathing hard.

"Me, either."

"Patty, let's not let this come between us."

The irony of his words struck her. "The problem was that nothing *did* come between us. Except a few clothes, but we'd have tossed those off in, oh, about ten seconds." Despite his earnest gaze, Patty put a little more space between them. "Let's face it, we should be past this, but at some level we're a pair of arrested adolescents."

"I need you. My daughter needs you." Alec began pacing. "This is my fault."

"Like you wrestled me to the ground and forced me to kiss your face off?" she scoffed.

"When we're together, I forget that things are different now, that this isn't just about you and me having fun," he admitted. "But I won't make that mistake again."

She shook her head. "Lost cause. I wish it weren't, but even after all these years we're still crazy together. You have to find someone else to protect your daughter. I'll explain to my boss."

Patty didn't look forward to *that* conversation. How was she going to admit she had an embarrassing weakness for an old flame? She hated to think of Mike gazing at her with a disappointed expression that reminded her of Grandpa.

But it could be much worse. What if she accepted this job and blew it because she couldn't focus one hundred percent on protecting Fiona? Her boss might decide she wasn't as qualified as he gave her credit for. And she'd have let everyone down.

Gripping her notepad tightly, Patty strode into the hall. Halfway across the living room, she heard a key turn in the lock.

Should have left five minutes ago.

She paused, holding steady as the door opened to reveal a birdlike woman. More wrinkles lined her inquisitive face than when Patty had last seen her, but the blue eyes remained just as penetrating.

Darlene Denny blinked in surprise. "Patty Hartman? My goodness."

"Hello, Mrs. Denny." Patty broke into a smile as a tiny figure pushed past her grandmother and ran over. "Good to see you, Fiona."

"Hi, Patty!" How could anyone resist that eager grin?

"You two have met?" A penciled eyebrow rose.

"I told you! The lady in the market. She has chocolate bars for dinner." Fiona jumped up and down. "Fried with sauce."

"If anyone could fry a chocolate bar, I'm sure it would be Patty." The woman sounded almost affectionate. Or possibly ironic.

"I was giving Alec a few tips on security." That seemed the easiest excuse for her presence. "On my way out." Patty wondered how awkward it would be to edge past Darlene. For such a small woman, she sure could block an exit.

"Nice tux," the older lady said. "I gather you were in the wedding party?"

"Maid of honor." In the awkward moment that followed, Patty wondered what you were supposed to say to the woman who'd separated you from the man you loved. *Stick to neutral topics.* "Guess you know the bride. Nora Kendall. Nora Franco now. She lives around here."

"Yes, I do know her. And, Patty?"

"Yes?" She registered Fiona flinging herself into Alec's arms. What a sweet pair. Honestly, who *were* they going to find to protect that child?

"It really is good to see you again," Mrs. Denny said.

Alec's train wreck of a marriage must make even his old girlfriend appealing. "Thanks. Good to see you, too."

Finally, Darlene moved aside and Patty barreled toward freedom. As she turned to wave goodbye, she snapped a mental image of Fiona sitting atop Alec's shoulders, the little girl's face alive with glee, the father's eyes pleading as they fixed on Patty.

Goodbye, goodbye. She went out and missed them already.

ALEC BARELY MANAGED to keep up with his daughter and mother's chatter about everything they'd done that day. Played board games, baked brownies, sung karaoke with a computer program and read books. *Flown to the moon, jumped into a lava pit...* He'd have bought anything, because he couldn't concentrate.

His body reverberated with the impact of holding Patty. Some vital part of him had burst out of hibernation and nearly attacked her. What was this power she had to arouse his wild instincts?

Disturbed though he was by his own behavior, he'd enjoyed being around her today. Her sense of humor energized him, and her honest, unfettered sexuality put manipulative kittens like Sabrina to shame.

Sabrina. Damn. How could he have let his impulses get in the way of protecting his daughter? Now he had to figure out how to lure Patty back.

Meanwhile, Tatum returned, and his mother and Fiona exclaimed over her new swimsuit, cover-up and other summer clothes. "I'm so pale. Everyone in the mall was staring at me." Tatum tugged her hair loose from its braid. The strands were falling out anyway, probably as a result of pulling so many garments over her head. "I don't look like a California girl."

"Tan skin isn't healthy," Alec replied automatically. "People should wear more sunscreen." He would have recited a few statistics about skin cancer, but the women were ignoring him. Besides, just because he worked in a hospital didn't mean he had to parrot good advice all the time.

"These are darling. You'll have a boyfriend in no time," Darlene said.

Tatum stuffed the clothes back into the bags. "I'm not cutting off the tags yet. I may return them. Shopping by myself, it was hard to tell what worked. It was fun to people-watch, though." She'd eaten dinner at the mall's food court, she explained.

"Will I get new clothes for my birthday?" Fiona asked.

"I'm sure you will. And afterward, I'll take you shopping for anything else you need." Alec knew from experience that Sabrina was likely to send new outfits, although her choices didn't always meet with his approval. In his view, little girls ought to dress like children, not miniature sex symbols. "Now, isn't it your bedtime?"

"I want to stay up." His daughter folded her arms stubbornly.

He should have known she'd be overtired and over-stimulated after such a busy day. "Please go put on your jammies."

"No! I want to stay up and talk to Tatum!" Fiona appeared on the verge of a tantrum.

The nanny intervened smoothly. "Why don't you get ready, and then I'll read to you."

"You're off duty," Alec pointed out.

"I don't mind." Tatum gave him a wistful smile. "I haven't had anyone to talk to all day except salesclerks. I'd enjoy the company." Taking the little girl's hand, she grabbed the bags with the other and off they went.

He remembered what Patty had said about swapping bedrooms. Well, tomorrow was soon enough. "I'll join you in a few minutes."

"Okay, Daddy," Fiona called back.

Darlene sat on a padded chair and rubbed her ankle. "That was fun, but exhausting."

"You want me to walk you to your place?" He'd never worried about his mother's safety on the stairs or the elevator, until he'd seen the place through Patty's eyes.

"I want you to explain why you had a police officer in a tuxedo giving you tips on security—or was that an excuse for inviting her over?"

"She isn't a police officer anymore. She's a private detective." Alec saw no point in beating around the bush. "I was hoping to hire her but I scared her off."

"You did, or me?" Darlene asked.

"Me. She was about to leave when you got here." He clamped his jaw shut, unwilling to explain further.

Darlene didn't pry. "I used to consider her a questionable influence, but I liked her, all the same. And compared to Sabrina, she's an angel. Private detective, huh?"

"I know you don't like the idea of a guard...."

"She's perfect. Hire her, at least for the birthday party." His mother flexed the ankle and winced. "It would be just like Sabrina to show up and make a scene."

He should have mentioned the upcoming party to Patty. "I suspect I didn't make things sound urgent enough. If she realized there could be a threat next weekend..."

"What kind of threat?"

He hadn't heard Tatum come in. Now the nanny stood regarding him with a pronounced pucker between her eyebrows. The sound of running water from the bathroom indicated Fiona's whereabouts.

"My ex-wife demanded an unsupervised visit with our daughter, and when I refused, she threatened to take her to Argentina." Much as he hated to alarm the nanny, she had a right to know the whole story. "I'm looking into hiring a security guard."

Tatum stared at him in alarm. "Do you know anything about that man she's dating?"

"I believe his family owns a manufacturing company." All the same, he supposed he ought to research Eduardo Patron, since the man might someday become Fiona's stepfather.

The nanny's chest rose and fell rapidly, as if she were on the verge of hyperventilating. "I didn't sign up to get in the middle of a kidnapping."

"Please don't make too much of this. It's probably an idle threat," Alec assured her.

"Besides, he's hiring a former policewoman to protect Fiona," Darlene interjected, ignoring the fact that Patty had turned down the job. "I know her personally. She'll be great."

Tatum glanced toward the hallway. The water had stopped running. "If you say so." She headed back to her charge.

"I'm afraid it won't take much to send that girl scurrying home to Boston," Darlene murmured.

Alec feared the same thing. Losing Tatum would be more than a mere inconvenience. Continuity of care was important to a child.

He had to change Patty's mind. He had logic on his side, since she'd already surveyed the premises and sketched the layout. Surely she wouldn't want to waste all that work.

He decided to make her a proposition: guard duty for a few days, and putting together a report with security recommendations. No private time with him. No bedroom encounters, no stolen kisses, no temptation.

Alec's hands tightened in anger, more at himself than at his ex-wife. How could he have forgotten, even for a moment, that Fiona's safety came first?

The sooner he made his case to Patty, the better. In a small town like Safe Harbor, it shouldn't be hard to find out where she lived. Come to think of it, she'd mentioned renting Leo Franco's house, and Alec had Tony Franco's cell-phone number. He'd give the attorney a call.

"I'll talk to Patty tomorrow," he promised his mother.

"She'll come around." She seemed utterly confident.

Alec hoped she was right. Now he intended to stick to his regular routine and read his daughter a bedtime story. Fiona had had more than enough disruptions for one day.

WHACK! The bank shot careened off the edge of the pool table, hit two other billiard balls and missed the pocket entirely.

Patty hated being off her game, even when she was alone. Why did Leo have to go off on his honeymoon and waste a perfect Sunday morning for their big match? She'd taken quite a few bets yesterday—maybe not the brightest idea, since Leo was one heckuva pool player, but it would be fun.

Not going to happen today, she reflected, and sank the next couple of balls with smooth calculation.

She almost wished she hadn't wrapped up so many cases this week, because she had nothing to do today. After years of working rotating shifts on patrol, Patty wasn't accustomed to having weekends off. Well, she hadn't had the *entire* weekend off, since she'd worked yesterday afternoon, but that had been fun. Aside from the elbow-in-the-face part, but the bruise hurt only when she laughed.

A smart police officer or detective avoided physical confrontations as much as possible. Still, there was something about being in the middle of the action that made her feel truly alive. After college, when she hadn't immediately been able to land a job on a police force, she'd considered enlisting in the military to follow in her grandpa's footsteps. He'd have liked that. But Drew had beaten her to the punch, and Patty hated coming in second to her kid brother.

She should have enlisted sooner. That would have proved to her grandpa that she wasn't a weakling like her mother. Sometimes she used to catch him watching her uneasily, as if just waiting for her to screw up.

Patty still cringed at the memory of his displeasure when he'd seen a D on an English paper she'd brought home the first semester of her senior year. Too much partying, too much moping after Alec. In her grandfather's eyes, she'd read the thought that she was headed straight downhill, like his own daughter.

Patty had buckled down and brought up her grades. When he saw them, he'd given a tight nod as if to say, *Well, you pulled it off this time.*

Sometimes she still felt as if she was proving her worth. To Mike. To Grandpa's stern ghost. And mostly to herself.

The doorbell rang. She gripped the cue, all fired up and ready for action. No one was going to get the drop on Patty Hartman.

Annoyed, she forced herself to ease off. She was living in a two-bedroom house in a cozy beach town where, on a Sunday morning, the worst-case scenario might be overly pushy missionaries at the front door.

All the same, she took the stick with her.

THE CRACKING SOUNDS FROM within made Alec hesitate on the doorstep. Patty must be playing pool solo, since he didn't see any other cars in front of the house, but the hard, thunking noises didn't bode well as to her mood. This was exactly the kind of defender Fiona needed, though: determined and fierce.

He rang the bell. A moment later, the door opened onto an unadorned entryway. To one side, Patty poised, half-shielded by the door, pool cue in hand.

"It's just me," Alec said.

Steady gray eyes took in his short-sleeved shirt and pressed jeans. "How do you manage that?"

"What?"

"To wear old grubbies like they were a Brooks Brothers suit." She gestured at her own loose T-shirt above a pair of work pants frayed around the hems.

"When my clothes get worn, I give them to the poor," he said. "Are you going to let me in or do I need to go roll in the mud first?"

As she moved back, he noticed the slim shape of her bare

feet, and when she turned, the way the oversize shirt clung to her breasts made his body tighten. *Stop that.*

"What brings you here this fine morning, Dr. Denny?" she inquired coolly.

"Please don't use the doctor thing." He instantly regretted the edge to his voice. But did he have to feel so aware of her as a woman? If it took a trace of irritability to keep her and his own reactions at bay, fine.

"Don't worry. I'm not going to faint into your arms and beg for mouth-to-mouth. Besides, as Mike told you, CPR is our department." She closed the door, revealing a Spartan living room in which a worn couch and chairs faced a large TV screen. The setup was perfect for watching ball games, and there was nothing on the coffee table but a couple of mug-shaped rings.

"This place suits you." When was the last time he'd simply hung out, losing track of time and forgetting about looming responsibilities? But he'd taken on his responsibilities willingly. And, in Fiona's case, with his entire heart and soul.

"This is mostly Leo's stuff, from before he moved in with Nora." Patty padded ahead of him into the kitchen and indicated a half-full pot of coffee. "Care for some?"

"No, thanks. I won't be staying long. I'm here on business." Yet, in this relaxed setting, the little speech he'd prepared about them both being professionals seemed stuffy and unconvincing.

"Yeah?" Patty's mouth worked expressively.

Her mouth had always been one of her best features. Last night, he'd thrashed around in bed all night, dreaming of her heated eagerness and passionate kiss. *And you are not going to think about that again.*

"I want to hire you. So does my mother," Alec blurted.

"Did your mommy write a note?"

"Yes," he retorted. "It says, 'Dear Miss Hartman, the

Denny family requests the honor of your services at my grand-daughter's birthday party next Saturday at Krazy Kids Pizza.' That's where Sabrina's most likely to make her move. Also, our nanny freaked out when she heard there was a threat. We really need you, even if it's just through next weekend. And those notes you took yesterday—you're halfway to putting together a plan already. Just a few days, that's all I'm asking."

He paused to catch his breath. Funny how he could supervise a complex scientific organization and deal with a difficult, abrasive boss, but barely kept from fidgeting beneath Patty's skeptical stare.

"Your mother agreed to hire me?" she said.

"She thinks you're perfect for the job. So do I."

For half a minute, Patty appeared to mull it over. "Cancel the pizza party," she said.

"I beg your pardon?"

She shrugged. "You wanted my advice."

He hadn't come here to be dismissed so lightly, especially with his daughter's safety at stake. Abruptly, Alec lost his taste for humoring Patty. "If you refuse to work for me, that's your choice. But I expect to be treated with common courtesy."

As they faced off across the linoleum, he caught a familiar pugnacious set to her shoulders, and had a brief mental image of Patty launching herself forward and tackling him. Well, let her try. A flip remark like that was uncalled for, and he intended to stand his ground.

"I'll take the job," she said. "Through next weekend, anyway."

He wasn't sure he'd heard correctly. "You will?"

"If you cancel the party," Patty amended.

"You were serious about that?"

"A pizza place is wide-open. No way to secure it, even with Mike on hand. If your ex intends to make trouble, especially if she brings help, we can't be everywhere at once."

He'd misjudged her comment, Alec realized. He should have known Patty wasn't simply yanking his chain. "How about if we move it instead of canceling?"

"There's a private clubhouse at your condo complex," she said. "That should work."

"I'll see if it's available. If not, we'll hold the party at my place." He could handle half a dozen tykes for one afternoon.

"I'll arrange for Mike to come with me tomorrow to take another look around. We'll go over our plan then. Any chance your mother and the nanny could be there, too?"

"Mom wouldn't miss it. As for Tatum, she has a low tolerance for scary topics. It's better if I fill her in later." He felt as if he was racing to keep up with this rapid flow of requests.

"Let me check Mike's schedule and get back to you." Patty reached out and shook his hand. Firmly. Impersonally.

Pleased as he was by this development, Alec wished to understand it. "What changed your mind?"

"About what?"

"Working for me."

Patty regarded him with a level expression. This was Officer Hartman, or, rather, Detective Hartman, Alec thought, struck by how little he knew his old friend, after all.

"For one thing, that pizza-party plan demonstrated that you people have no idea how to guard against a possible abduction," she responded.

"What's the other thing?"

She gave a faint smile. "If your mother really did request me, I wouldn't want her to think I hold grudges."

"Glad to hear it." Alec would have enjoyed lingering, but he'd learned that once you negotiated an agreement, it was time to leave. No hanging around, no snatching defeat from the jaws of victory. "See you tomorrow."

"I'll call you in the morning to set a time."

So this was the new Patty, he mused as he went down the steps between neatly clipped bushes. Across the street, a teenage boy pushed a lawn mower noisily over the grass. Two little girls skipped rope while a terrier darted around them, yipping excitedly.

Alec wasn't convinced Patty had told him the whole story about why she'd changed her mind. He was just grateful that she had.

Chapter Nine

By early Monday evening, when Patty and Mike met with Alec and his mother, they'd prepared a list of recommendations broken down into categories. Immediate steps—changing the alarm codes, rekeying locks and coordinating with condo management and security—were only the beginning.

To Patty's satisfaction, Alec assured her he'd reported his ex-wife's threat to the police. They'd asked him to keep them informed if she did anything else suspicious.

After visiting the clubhouse, which turned out to be available on Saturday, the four of them toured the premises and repaired to Darlene's unit. Meeting there allowed Fiona and Tatum to stay undisturbed at home, and gave Patty a chance to assess the downstairs condo, which needed a stronger lock on the sliding patio door.

Now, sitting on the flowery furniture amid the scent of sweet rolls Darlene had baked for them, Patty watched Alec's reaction during Mike's presentation. A muscle quirking in his jaw, he listened intently, taking it all in with the keenness of a father preparing to defend his young.

She'd never thought of Alec as a warrior, but while he certainly lacked formal training, she had no doubt that he'd leap to take action. Much as she admired his devotion, she was glad when Mike said, "Whichever one of us, Patty or I, is present when anything occurs, you and everyone else should follow our lead. No matter how much you want to play hero, don't. That's our job."

Darlene nodded, wide-eyed. Alec considered for a moment before he, too, conceded.

Mike continued with their list. He planned to meet with the complex's manager, ensure that landscapers and other workmen were screened and coordinate with the condo's security personnel. In addition to conducting random patrols to watch for suspicious activity, he and Patty would talk to the neighbors. "Not only do they need to know who we are and why we're here, they're on the premises 24/7. They can be our eyes and ears."

Darlene gave a small shudder. To her credit, she accepted their expertise and didn't ask if this was really necessary.

"I've done some preliminary checking on Eduardo Patron," Mike went on, his tall frame nearly overwhelming one of the delicate chairs. Normally, he wouldn't have done this much work without first receiving a retainer, but he'd picked up Patty's concern and had pressed ahead. "He appears to be a legitimate businessman with a colorful personal life. His wife, Paloma, is a former TV actress with a hot temper, and he's had a couple of affairs. This appears to be the first time he's sought a divorce, though."

"If Sabrina does manage to take Fiona to Argentina, do you think this woman might get violent? Toward Fiona, I mean?" Darlene obviously didn't care about any risk to her ex-daughter-in-law.

"No telling, but we'll do our best to keep it from going that far," Mike assured her. "My question is whether Sabrina Denny might harm her own daughter, accidentally or otherwise."

That she might was hard for Patty to imagine, but Alec looked uncertain. "I don't believe she'd intentionally hurt Fiona, but there's no telling what she might do. Given the way she endangered our daughter once..." He trailed off, obviously disturbed by the memory.

"She fits right in with this guy Patron's taste in women. One of his former lovers was a Peruvian newswoman who attacked him with scissors when he broke up with her," Mike said. "Made the newspapers down there."

"I don't understand why Sabrina's making such an issue of getting her hands on Fiona." Darlene pushed through the quaver in her voice. "It's not as if she's much of a mother."

"I long ago stopped trying to understand people's behavior in divorce situations," Mike admitted.

Patty had an idea of how the woman might be thinking. "This Eduardo character appears to have a short attention span. With his wife screaming bloody murder, Sabrina may be grasping for a way to draw his attention back to herself."

"You mean she's putting my granddaughter in jeopardy just to stir things up with her boyfriend?" Darlene's face puckered as if she'd like to bite someone, and there was no question about who that someone was.

"I wouldn't put it past her," Alec muttered tightly.

"On the plus side, we don't seem to be dealing with professional criminals, although we can't rule out the possibility that she'll hire someone," Mike went on in his usual steady tone. "On the downside, she's unpredictable. Still, this isn't the movies—she's not going to parachute onto the roof. From a practical standpoint, we need to assess when your daughter will be most vulnerable."

Alec leaned forward. He'd come straight from work, wearing tailored slacks and a button-down shirt open at the throat. Remembering the hardness of his chest as she'd stroked it the other night, Patty had to tear her gaze away.

"I switched her bedroom with Tatum's, as Patty recommended," he said. "What else should we worry about?"

Patty took the lead for this part of the presentation, as she and Mike had planned. "Anytime she's away from home, someone could grab her. Playing in a park, shopping, getting in and out of the car."

"We can't lock her up!" Darlene protested.

"If there's an immediate threat, that's exactly what we'd advise," Mike told her. "It's up to Dr.—excuse me, Mr. Denny—to determine how much risk he's willing to take."

"I'd like to hire Patty to accompany Fiona whenever she's off the premises," Alec replied thoughtfully. "At least for the next week, until we see how this plays out."

That meant spending a lot of time with the little girl. Patty actually looked forward to it, and fortunately, she doubted she'd need to be alone with Alec. Because no matter how hard she concentrated, she always felt a subtle hum of awareness in his presence.

"Also, be careful whenever she moves between your condo and your mother's," Patty warned. "When I'm not around, it would be best to keep her on the second floor exclusively. And we'll have to teach her to take precautions. It's a good idea for children to learn some basic self-protection rules, anyway."

"She's an innocent little kid. I hate having to do this." Alec's fists clenched and unclenched. "Are you sure this isn't too much?"

"That's up to you to decide," Mike said. "But I recommend that we start immediately."

Alec took only a second to think it over. "All right. Even if it's overkill, it's worth it."

From his briefcase, Mike produced a contract. Although Alec blanched when he saw the cost, he raised no objection. After signing the form, he wrote a check for what Patty knew must be a substantial amount.

"I'll go liaise with condo management while Patty talks to your daughter and her nanny." After rising, Mike shook hands all around. "Mrs. Denny, please take extra precautions for your own safety. Call upstairs to let them know when you're coming, and also when you return safely to your condo. Check the elevator and the stairwell before exiting public view."

Darlene's hand fluttered to her chest. "You think I might be in danger?"

"There's a chance Sabrina might confront you in some way," Mike said. "Do you live alone here? Patty mentioned a housekeeper. What hours does she work?"

Alec looked exasperated. "That's an ongoing problem. Marla has health issues, and she's sent a series of nieces in her stead. They haven't been particularly reliable."

"Not a good situation—" Mike started to say, until Darlene waved her hand, as if asking permission to speak. "Yes, Mrs. Denny?"

"In all the excitement, I forgot to mention that Marla called yesterday to say she's sending her cousin Rosita. She apologized for all the problems and said Rosita's very mature and experienced. She starts day after tomorrow."

"On Wednesday? That's good news. At least, I hope so." Alec didn't sound convinced.

"That's another issue—background checks," Mike said. "We can run those on your staff and the people close to you."

"Whatever you think is necessary." Alec got to his feet. "Let's not delay any longer. Tatum's supposed to be off duty, and I hate taking advantage of her."

Within minutes, Patty and Alec were on their way upstairs. She was glad to hear Darlene locking the dead bolt behind them.

"This situation doesn't quite feel real to me," Alec admitted as he followed Patty up the steps.

"You're not used to it. I am." She kept her eyes forward, trying not to think about how appealing he'd looked downstairs with his shirt collar open and his slim-fitting pants emphasizing the hard length of his legs. For the duration of this assignment, he was the client. Nothing more and nothing less.

"You like this kind of work?" he asked.

"I like protecting people." She paused at a movement on the second-floor walkway. A teenage boy, backpack in place, was letting himself out of a unit. "Hey," he said as he passed them, and Patty responded in kind.

She didn't see anyone else around, and Alec had to undo a dead bolt to get inside. So far, so good.

But with his ex-wife involved in a soap-opera relationship, Patty didn't discount anything. Up to and including parachutes on the roof.

DESPITE PATTY'S EFFORT to explain their plans in a nonthreatening manner, Alec could tell things weren't going well with Tatum.

Already tired from spending the day switching bedrooms, the nanny wore an uneasy expression as she learned that she'd have a bodyguard with her whenever she and Fiona went out. "What about when I'm alone?" she demanded. "Your ex-wife knows me on sight."

In the two years since Alec had gained custody, Sabrina had bristled on the few occasions when Tatum was around during supervised visits, as if the nanny were somehow partly responsible for the situation. Sabrina never hesitated to take out her ill temper on whoever was nearby, and she'd homed in on this vulnerable target. After a few unpleasant encounters, Alec had made sure Tatum was elsewhere whenever his ex-wife made an appearance.

"After this weekend, I suspect her mother will have other things on her mind," he told the young woman, who was tugging uneasily at her thick braid.

Fiona hugged her favorite stuffed bunny. "Mommy's coming to my party, isn't she?"

"She might." The custody order allowed Sabrina to see her daughter on her birthday, so Alec could hardly forbid it, but visits with Sabrina were uncertain affairs, with frequent delays and no-shows. Still, he understood that his little girl loved her mother. "And Fiona, we're going to have it here at the clubhouse instead of Krazy Kids Pizza."

His daughter stared at him in distress. "But you promised! I want clowns and games!"

"We'll have better games." His mother had promised to call a party planner in the morning. *Please let somebody be available on short notice.*

"I want my pizza party!" Fiona cried with all the pent-up emotion of a child who, Alec had to admit, had been through a lot. She'd been forced out of her bedroom today, on top of the recent move away from her friends. While he and Darlene had managed to invite a few children for Saturday, she scarcely knew them.

"I'll make balloon animals," Tatum promised.

"I want my pizza party!" Fiona had latched on to a theme and she was sticking to it.

Tatum's eyes glistened. "I'm sorry I can't be more helpful," she told Alec, "but this is more than I bargained for."

"I'm sorry for all the extra demands we've placed on you." He tried to sound soothing despite his ragged mood. Mostly he was furious with his ex-wife for creating so much trouble. "You've gone above and beyond the call of duty."

"Take a break," Patty advised the nanny. "We'll deal with this."

With a short nod, Tatum fled down the hall. Alec heard her go into a bedroom, then come out and go into another one. Still unused to the change.

Fiona's lower lip quivered mutinously. "My party! You promised, Daddy!"

"I know, but…" *But I'd do anything in the world to keep you safe. Even make you angry with me.*

Patty knelt on the carpet by Fiona's chair. "Aren't you going to introduce me to your bunny?"

The little girl regarded her suspiciously. Finally, she said, "This is Hoppity."

"What's wrong with his ear?" Solemnly, Patty examined the frayed rabbit.

"It's busted. Me and Tatum patched it." She sent a quick glance at Alec. "I mean, Tatum and me."

Still ungrammatical, but right now, he couldn't have cared less.

"Looks like the Band-Aid's coming off." Patty indicated the nearly unfastened patch. "Hoppity needs surgery. That's the only permanent cure."

What was she getting at? If this was a ploy to short-circuit his daughter's hysteria, it could backfire. Fiona wasn't a two-year-old with a short attention span.

"You mean like in a hospital?" Fiona regarded Patty curiously.

"Yes." Patty set the bunny back in the little girl's arms. "I saw an article in the newspaper once about a teddy bear clinic to help children feel comfortable visiting the doctor. We could do something like that for your party."

"A teddy bear clinic?" That was a great idea. Alec had to give Patty credit, too, for taking his daughter's feelings seriously. "I could round up bandages and other supplies."

"It would be good to have a nurse in uniform. Think Bailey would do it?" Patty asked.

He nodded, relief flooding him. One minute, he'd been dreading the event, and now he could see how much fun they'd have. "We'll invite the other kids to bring their old stuffed animals."

"Can we run tests like you do, Daddy?" Fiona asked.

"You bet." He would figure something out. Hmm. Teddy bear infertility—could be an emerging medical field.

"I bet you could learn to suture." Patty raised her eyebrows at Alec. "She's old enough to use a needle, isn't she?"

"I'd say so."

"Yeah!" The little girl bounced up and down.

As ideas poured forth, Alec jotted a few notes. It was an excited little girl who finally donned her jammies and got tucked into bed. To Alec's surprise, she demanded a night-night book from Patty instead of him.

He indicated a row of his daughter's favorites, but Patty waved them away. "I'd rather tell a story than read one. Okay?"

"Okay!" Fiona buried her nose into the bunny as if drawing comfort from its familiar scent.

Patty settled on the edge of the bed. Seated in an old rocking chair, Alec noted how the lamplight made a halo of her blond hair. In the old days, he'd been intrigued by the contrasts in her nature, the way she would leap at physical challenges regardless of risk, then melt into his arms. Now, he saw how much she'd mellowed—and yet she hadn't lost her passion for life.

"Once upon a time, there was a little girl who lived with her brother, Drew, and two mixed-up parents," Patty began.

"Mixed up how?" Fiona asked.

"They lived in a messy apartment and sometimes forgot to cook dinner for their children," she said.

She was telling her own story, Alec realized. Edited version, suitable for a child to hear. Considering that, as far as he knew, Patty hadn't spent much time around kids, she had a lot of sensitivity.

"Did they do dumb things like my mommy sometimes?"

"They did," Patty said. "So this little girl and her brother went to live with their grandfather, who used to be a soldier and had a very neat house."

"Did he ever shoot anybody?" Fiona never lacked for questions.

"If he did, he didn't talk about it." Patty tugged the covers into place over the wriggly child. "It was hard on the little girl because she missed her parents, even though they had problems, and her grandpa was very strict. She had to get used to a new room, and she missed her old friends. But she had to be strong for her brother. It helps when you have somebody to take care of."

Fiona clutched the stuffed animal. "Like Hoppity?"

"Exactly," Patty said. "After a while, this little girl got used to living with her grandfather. Even when her parents cleaned up their act, the little girl and her brother stayed with Grandpa. And they lived happily ever after."

Alec waited to see how his daughter would react. At four-going-on-five, she often came up with reactions that surprised him.

Sure enough, after a moment, she said, "What happened to her really?"

"She grew up to be me," Patty replied. "I was a police officer for a while and now I'm in private security. I protect people, and for the next week or so, I'm going to be protecting you."

"Why do you have to protect me?"

Alec wished they didn't have to explain this to Fiona, yet if he shielded her too much, she'd be defenseless. She had to learn that adults, even those you loved, didn't automatically deserve your trust.

Patty appeared to be choosing her words carefully. "Your

mommy misses you and she might try to take you away from your daddy. But she's not supposed to do that."

"Because the court said so?"

"That's right. So if she or anyone else takes you with them, run away. If for any reason we aren't around, go inside a store, or find a policeman, or ask a lady with children to help you. Tell them you've been kidnapped."

"Okay." Two little arms lifted for a hug. Without hesitation, Patty drew her close. Alec could have sworn he saw a glimmer of moisture in his old friend's eyes, but it might have been a trick of the light.

After he'd hugged his daughter, too, he and Patty went out. Down the hall, Tatum's door was shut. He could hear her on the phone. The words were indistinct but he noted anxiety in her voice.

Patty glanced toward Fiona's room. "She's adorable."

"She's everything." Alec barely resisted a desire to go take another look, as if his daughter might have vanished the moment he stepped out. "I'm surprised you haven't had one or two of your own by now." No sooner had the words left his mouth than he wondered why he'd uttered them.

"Me?" Patty's eyebrows went up. "Hey, kids are cute, but not really my style. I mean, where would I stash one while I'm working?"

"You'd do the same thing a guy does. Find someone you can trust to handle child care."

"Huh." With that cryptic comment, she drew out her pad. "Let's plan my schedule for the week. What time do you usually leave for work? What do Fiona and Tatum and your mom do all day?"

He filled her in as much as he could, and arranged for her to return the next morning to confer with the nanny and

Darlene on timing. Once they settled into their new routine, Alec told himself, he'd stop worrying about every detail.

But until he resolved this danger from his ex-wife, he'd never rest easy.

Chapter Ten

Although Patty kept tabs on a couple of other cases that week, she spent most of her energy arranging Fiona's protection. On the surface, everything went smoothly. The neighbors were glad to cooperate, Darlene kept her doors locked and Tatum notified Patty whenever they planned to leave the premises. During their trips to the playground and a children's museum, Fiona gladly joined in the game of watching for anyone or anything suspicious.

It seemed as if their efforts might be unnecessary. Sabrina had phoned again from New York to demand that her daughter visit her. "Eduardo's wife keeps threatening to show up and raise a stink. How can I leave at a time like this?"

"You can celebrate her birthday later. Surely you don't want her there when Mrs. Patron arrives," Alec reported telling her.

He'd done a great job mimicking his wife's shrill voice, as well.

"Eduardo might have some business in L.A., so maybe we'll come, after all. I have the right to see her on her birthday."

Alec had conceded the point. And yet, he told Patty, his wife hadn't seemed happy about his acquiescence, either. Obviously, the woman didn't want a solution, she wanted attention.

In the meantime, plans for the teddy bear clinic moved

forward so well that Darlene decided against hiring a party planner. Her new housekeeper, Rosita, proved as skilled and dependable as promised, and spoke excellent English with a light, pleasant accent. Although she'd recently moved to the area from Houston and needed Darlene's instructions on where to shop for decorations and refreshments, she pitched in with a will.

"I keep my eyes open for trouble," she promised Patty. "Any problems, I call you."

Still, no matter how well matters were falling into place, Patty couldn't dismiss the possibility of some slip up. She kept remembering when she was thirteen and Grandpa had left for a military reunion, trusting her to watch ten-year-old Drew for the weekend. She'd planned meals, organized homework and set strict rules, but the next afternoon her brother fell while in-line skating and broke his arm. Forced to return early, their tight-lipped grandfather hadn't assigned blame, yet his disapproval had reverberated through Patty for weeks. It didn't matter who was at fault, or if no one was. She'd still let him down.

There was always one thing you didn't foresee, one flaw that no one considered. She couldn't allow that to happen. Especially not to Fiona.

Those melting brown eyes. That habit of thinking things over and trying to see inside them. The sudden flashes of vulnerability when Patty least expected it.

Just like Alec.

Patty knew what Grandpa would say: that she was an idiot to have feelings for a man who'd treated her so shabbily. That she risked letting him and the child and herself down if she didn't stay focused. That emotions made you weak.

She wished she had a close girlfriend to talk things over with. Given Patty's inclination to go target shooting or play pool in her free time, she rarely hung out with other women.

When she did make friends, they always seemed to move away or get involved with a guy, and that was the end of that.

So when Bailey, who'd agreed to play nurse at Saturday's party, suggested they meet for lunch at the hospital cafeteria on Thursday, Patty quickly accepted. Not that she planned to reveal much about her confused feelings, especially considering how freely her old high-school chum chattered, but just being around another woman might help put things in perspective.

After parking at the hospital, Patty texted Tatum to confirm she and Fiona were at home, giving stuffed animals their annual physicals as a practice for Saturday.

Bunny in bed w temp, Tatum sent back. Panda arm healing.

Fiona? Patty tapped.

Xray kit. In other words, taking digital photos of her third-favorite plush toy, KitKat.

Gd wrk! C U ltr.

Satisfied about the pair's safety, Patty sauntered through the hospital lobby and down a short hallway to the cafeteria. She'd eaten here occasionally while visiting hospitalized friends, and enjoyed the array of serving stations with hot and cold dishes.

From a corner table, Bailey waved. Pregnancy agreed with her, Patty observed as she grabbed a corned-beef sandwich and got in line for the cashier. Her old friend's short brown hair seemed thick and glossy, and her freckled cheeks shone with good health.

"I bet she keeps you busy." Patty scooted into a seat.

"I sure hope we can find someone to fill in during her maternity leave. Maybe she won't take much time off." Bailey had a knack for downing bites of food with scarcely a pause in the flow of words. "Maybe Dr. Brennan will join us. I hear she wants to move her practice to Safe Harbor."

Chewing her sandwich, Patty merely nodded. How did a person work the topic around to what really interested her, which was how to sort out inappropriate romantic impulses?

Bailey chattered on. "But I'd hate having to work for Dr. Tartikoff. I hear he's an arrogant pain in the neck. He'll probably bring his nurse with him from Boston. He obviously likes to have his own staff around him, like Alec."

Patty's ears pricked. The trouble was, she didn't want to talk about Alec. Not specifically. Her goal was to figure out, without naming names, how to stop fantasizing about a man she had to work with.

Hopeless. Ridiculous. And, of course, by now Bailey had moved right along to another subject. The names *Phyllis* and *Boone* jumped out at Patty. They, she recalled, would be the sister and brother-in-law.

"...cash-flow problems," Bailey was saying. "I know it's part of running their own company, and investments are never a sure thing, but I didn't expect to be fronting the money for some of my medical costs."

That sounded wrong to Patty. "You're the surrogate. They should be covering everything."

"Absolutely, and they will. But..." Her friend paused to wave at a couple of women approaching with trays.

Patty felt a jolt of dismay at the possibility that these new arrivals might decide to join them, and sent them a mental push. It must have worked, because they went on out to the cafeteria patio.

"In the meantime, I can't let the bills pile up," Bailey added. "Hurting their credit rating isn't going to help the business."

"You said they'd invested your savings," Patty reminded her. "What are you paying the bills with?"

"I always keep enough cash on hand to cover expenses for

three months. Unfortunately, it's down to one month at this point." The nurse's hand drifted to her slightly rounded abdomen. "Oh, darn. I thought that might be movement, but it's just my stomach grumbling. I can't wait to feel the baby!"

Much as she wanted to empathize, Patty couldn't take much interest in a pregnancy. It seemed alien, the idea of carrying another life inside her. Then again, what if that baby came out as cute as Fiona?

"Are there women who're better at parenting older kids?" she blurted. "I mean, I don't think I'm into diapers."

Bailey laughed. "Oh, Patty, you were never like other girls. I'm sure you'll find your own path."

Now, there was an opening, even if a slim one, to a discussion about relationships. "Being different isn't always a good thing. I mean, in high school, I never dated around like most girls, so I didn't learn much about boys. Other than Alec, obviously. I'm kind of ignorant for being almost thirty."

"But you work with guys," Bailey pointed out.

"That's different." Patty had listened to plenty of locker-room comments, but the guys hadn't said anything that would help her through the current circumstances.

"You must have dated some of them."

"A few. But nothing serious." *How could it be when I compared every guy to Alec?* Whoa! That was a scary thought. "How about you?"

"I got married at nineteen. We eloped." Patty stared into the distance as if picturing the guy's face. "He was cute, I was emotionally needy and running away to Las Vegas sounded romantic. How dumb is that? Neither of us had a clue about marriage. It's amazing we lasted two years. A year and a half, actually."

It struck Patty that she didn't have a clue about marriage, either. "What do you wish you'd known?"

"About marriage?"

"Yeah."

Bailey regarded her dubiously. "What do you mean?"

"I guess I'm asking what it takes to make a marriage work."

"I have no idea."

Well, *that* didn't help.

"I'll tell you what I've learned about guys, though," Bailey went on.

"Okay." Patty would settle for whatever pearls of wisdom she could gather, however random.

"Don't take your feelings too seriously. Just run with them. Fall in love, and when it's over, kiss the guy goodbye and move on," the nurse told her earnestly. "That's what men do, so why shouldn't we?"

"You don't miss any of them?" Patty asked.

"For about five minutes," Bailey said, raising her hands, palms out. "I allow myself two days to cry, and then it's done."

"You have ten fingers raised," Patty pointed out.

"That hand represents the last five guys I cried over," her friend replied. "Guy number one turned out to be married. Guy number two was practically a stalker—I had to get a court order. Guy number three…"

"Where do you find these losers and why do you bother?"

"They're everywhere. And I bother because I'd rather cry myself to sleep once in a while than give up on ever finding true love."

Patty tried to process that statement. "But you just said…"

"I'd like to experience true love, once," Bailey responded. "Yeah, it would hurt when it ended, but at least I'd know what it was like."

"If it ended, it wouldn't be true love."

"Sure it would. It would *feel* true."

"You never took any classes in logic, did you?" Patty had to chuckle at herself, asking advice from a woman who set land speed records for ending relationships.

"You should have a fling with Alec. That's the only way you'll ever get over him," Bailey stated.

"Say what?" She hadn't seen that conversational curve ball coming.

"Oh, come on. You've avoided each other since high school, and where did that get you? He's divorced and you're alone."

No use denying it. "Okay, I grant you, there's still some radioactive fallout from the nuclear blast twelve years ago," Patty said. "But we're in touch quite a bit right now, as you're aware. And nothing's happening, nor should it."

"But you've got the hots for him," Bailey finished for her.

Patty's cheeks flushed. "Is it that obvious?"

"Only to me." The nurse began stacking their empty dishes. "My advice is, don't confine yourself to guard-dog duty. Slip the guy off his leash once in a while. Remember, the only way to disperse radiation is to vent it into the atmosphere."

Patty struggled to grasp all those images. Dogs, leashes, radiation. "Uh, I'll try."

"And remember, when it's over, cry for two days and move on." The nurse got to her feet.

"Even for true love?" Patty teased.

"Maybe three or four. See you Saturday!" Bailey carried her tray to the conveyer belt.

That had to be the worst advice Patty had ever received, but her friend's words did contain one grain of truth. Ignoring each other hadn't made the attraction end.

She checked her watch. Nothing scheduled until three,

when Darlene planned to take Tatum and Fiona to the library. Patty had one other case pending. It involved a runaway teenage boy who she was fairly certain was hanging out at an older friend's place. Since she'd had no luck catching him during daylight hours, she planned to cruise by there after dark.

That left her in the same building as Alec with a free hour or so. While he'd assured her and Mike they didn't need to evaluate his workplace security, she'd like to get a sense of the area all the same.

She texted him, and received an immediate reply: Cm down 2 my lair.

His lair? Without giving herself a chance to consider the implications, Patty skimmed down the stairs—none of that elevator nonsense—to the hospital's basement. Alec had explained that he was renovating a large basement storage facility into several related labs. They would be used for storing and processing eggs and sperm, and creating babies in test tubes or their high-tech equivalent. It sounded like mad scientist stuff from those B-grade science fiction movies they used to love.

Patty couldn't wait to see what he was up to. All the same, she felt a twinge of disappointment at emerging into a well-lit corridor. No monsters or bloodsucking blobs in sight, although the cool air did raise goose bumps along her arms.

The rumble of wheels was all the warning she received before a refrigerator came trundling around a corner on a dolly, pushed by a workman. "Sorry," he said as she jumped back. "Wasn't expecting to see anyone."

She shouldn't have dismissed the dangers so lightly—a person could suffer a seriously barked shin around here. "I'm looking for Alec Denny."

"Follow me." He took off, hurrying past a chamber from which issued loud clanking noises. Patty peered through the open doorway, hoping for a glimpse of something exotic, robotic or hypnotic, but all she saw was a workman installing pipes.

Farther along the hallway, her guide gestured into a room. Here, work had progressed much further. The floor and ceiling looked finished, and the walls were lined with industrial-style freezers, refrigerators and neatly stacked metal containers that to Patty resembled washer-dryers.

"Over here," called a familiar voice. From the side, Alec shot her a boyish grin that took the edge off the chill. On his blue blazer, a tag displayed his name and the title Director of Laboratories.

"Dr. Frankenstein, I presume?" she asked.

"*Ja, Fräulein,* here ve create life from de ooze." Chuckling, Alec helped the workman unload the refrigerator into one of the few unoccupied spaces along the wall. "Isn't this place amazing?"

"Yeah," she said. "It's definitely you."

He'd shown her his bedroom once during high school—Darlene hadn't been keen on letting Patty into that particular part of the house, she recalled—so she could see how he'd equipped it as a lab. There'd been a table with a microscope, shelves of insect specimens and petri dishes, even a small refrigerator because, he'd explained, his mother wasn't crazy about finding his biology experiments in with her food.

Here it was, the grown-up version, times a zillion. Alec's dream lab. "What are all these things?" She indicated the stacked equipment.

After thanking the workman and sending him along, Alec dusted off his hands. "Not a sterile environment yet, as you can see. Well, over there are cell freezers and over here are incubators. Once we're up and running, they'll hold eggs and embryos in a constant, clean environment."

"What do you mean by constant?"

"It means that we control the temperature and the composition of the air," he said.

With that, he was off and running on what was obviously his favorite subject. Well, second to his daughter. Eyes alight, Alec explained how separate labs would be dedicated to functions from analyzing sperm to what he called micromanipulation.

"Our ability to achieve fertilization even with less-than-optimal eggs and sperm is improving dramatically. You wouldn't believe how quickly the field has advanced," Alec told her. "We're gaining ground on preventing birth defects, too. We plan to participate in research projects to switch genes on and off using epigenetics."

"Epi what?" Patty had seen newspaper articles about the genetic studies underway at the University of California's nearby Irvine campus, but she didn't recall that term.

"It's one of the hottest fields in biology," Alex enthused. "You know people can have the same genes, like identical twins, but still be different in some ways? Or if you clone a cat, the genetic double may have different coloring?"

"Actually, I didn't know that." Patty couldn't see why anyone would clone a kitty, considering how many of them languished in shelters, longing for homes.

"It's because many of our gene functions can be turned on or off by the epigenome. I guess in simple terms you could call it a layer of biochemical reactions. So—"

"Those are simple terms?" Patty's head was whirling. "You left me back there with the cloned kittens."

"Sorry. I get carried away."

Carried away and vibrating with enthusiasm. It struck her that his work was Alec's true love. In a sense, this was what he'd left her for, not that she would have stood in his way. But he'd always possessed an inner drive that was destined to take him far beyond Patty and Safe Harbor.

Only now it had brought him back. Life was funny that way.

"You love this, don't you?" she said softly.

"It's..." His hands flexed, as if he couldn't wait to get them on a microscope, or whatever it was he used to do this micromanipulation business. "It's a miracle. Just to be part of it is such a privilege. I was lucky to hook up with someone as visionary as Owen Tartikoff."

"Bailey says he's a pain in the neck."

Alec burst out laughing and draped his arms over Patty's shoulders, facing her at nuzzling distance. "I can always count on you to bring me down to earth."

"Is that a good thing?" She was surprised at how wistful she sounded. "I wish I understood your work better." This was a key part of his life she'd never been able to share.

"I married a fellow biologist, and look where that got me," he answered, his forehead nearly touching hers.

"It got you Fiona."

At this close range, his eyes were huge and darkly inviting. "Like I said, I can always count on you to remind me of the things that really matter."

She supposed they were both, in their own way, helping and protecting people. They really did have a lot in common. Such as the desire to touch each other, she thought, and ran her palms down the sides of his blazer. "I never kissed a director of laboratories before."

His mouth grazed hers. "There. What do you think?"

"This requires further analysis," she said, and enjoyed the moist heat of his lips against hers as she drew him closer. Through her blouse and his shirt, she felt the hard thrum of his heart, powering them both. Yearning flooded her, and she grasped his hips, angling him against her, feeling his arousal.

"Patty, Patty," he whispered, lifting his head for a moment. "What are we going to do?"

Love each other and then cry for a few days? That might work for Bailey—although Patty had her doubts—but it certainly wouldn't work for them. "I don't know."

His cell rang in a distinctive tone. "It's Tatum. I'd better get that."

Patty stepped back, suddenly self-conscious. What were they doing, smooching like teenagers in his lab, where anyone might walk in? How unprofessional. Besides, she'd taken on the responsibility of protecting Alec's home and family, and she was doing a lousy job at the moment. She hadn't even made an attempt to assess the place.

Although he'd notified hospital security as she and Mike had requested, no one had checked Patty's ID on the way down. Suppose Sabrina went out of control and came here to wreak havoc? There might not be any embryos yet—when there were, no doubt the doors would be locked to protect the sterility, anyway—but this equipment must cost a fortune.

Still, the ex hadn't threatened Alec's work. And you couldn't guard every single aspect of his life without bringing in far more staff than he could afford.

"Please calm down. Tell me exactly what happened." His words drew her up sharply.

"Fiona?" Patty went on high alert. While she'd been fooling around, she'd left her charge unprotected.

He shook his head. A rush of relief ran through her. All the same, she should have been more careful.

"You're sure it was her?" he went on, still talking to the nanny. "Right, I forgot the land line has caller ID. Did Sabrina make any specific threat, or... I understand, but...I wish you'd reconsider. I'm coming home right now… Yes, of course." He frowned at the phone for a moment before clicking off.

"What is it?" Patty demanded.

Grimly, Alec stuck the cell in his pocket. "My ex called the condo. Whatever she said, it was enough to spook Tatum." His troubled gaze met Patty's. "She's quitting. As of right now."

Chapter Eleven

As he phoned to inform the receptionist that he'd been called away by a family emergency, it dawned on Alec what he had to do next. The question was how to persuade Patty, especially after their lapse a few minutes ago.

It hadn't felt like a lapse, though. It had brought home the fact that in all these years, he'd never felt complete without her. Having Patty around was a greater pleasure than he'd been willing to admit, but acting the way they had was wrong. Wrong for them and wrong for Fiona.

He couldn't afford to be selfish. He couldn't let his daughter down again. And his actions had been particularly ill judged in view of this unforeseen development.

"What's going on?" Patty strode beside him out of the lab.

"There's been another threat."

"We should bring in the police."

"Not that clear-cut a threat. Just enough to spook her." En route to the parking garage, he filled Patty in on the latest events.

Tatum had answered the home phone, to hear a woman's tight voice snarl, "Look out, you b—" followed by a hang-up. It might have been dismissed as a prank had the call display not identified Sabrina's cell number.

If not for the earlier threat to snatch Fiona, Alec might have been able to persuade Tatum to overlook it. Instead, she was probably online right now, reserving her flight to Boston.

That left him without full-time care for his daughter. Darlene might volunteer, but he didn't like imposing on her to that extent, especially in light of her recent injury. And he could hardly enroll his daughter in a preschool with this threat hanging over their heads.

Patty, who'd had no trouble matching his rapid pace, stopped beside his SUV. "The call came from Sabrina's cell, right? So she could be anywhere."

He registered that, indeed, his ex-wife might be lurking nearby. "That's true."

"Phone her," Patty said. "See what kind of shape she's in. Maybe you can get a sense of where she is and what she's up to."

He tried it. The call went directly to voice mail. He left a terse message for Sabrina to call him, *now.*

"Do you have a number for her home?"

He pressed that one, too. No answer. He left another message. "I'll try again later." It would be a relief to learn his ex was still in New York. If, indeed, she was.

"She's trying to shake you. Don't let her." Patty's piercing gaze fixed on him. "I'm parked one level up and I need to notify Mike, so I'll meet you at the condo. But first, take a few deep breaths. Focus on your driving. You're upset, and the last thing you need is to get into an accident."

Levelheaded Patty. Thank goodness for her ability to stay in the moment and think clearly. "I'll be careful."

She nodded. "See you in a few."

He caught her arm. "Wait. There's something we have to discuss, and we can't do it in front of my daughter."

Patty tilted her head, watching him from beneath a fringe of blond hair. "Mmm?"

She seemed so in control, despite everything. When had

his off-the-cuff high-school chum turned into such a rock? Alec hoped she wouldn't mind that he intended to lean on her a little further.

"I'd like you to take over for Tatum. Obviously, you aren't a nanny, but Fiona likes and trusts you. If you could watch her full-time for the next few days, I'd feel a lot better." Whatever this cost, it would be worth it.

Her skeptical expression didn't bode well. "I can watch her on a double shift, which ought to cover the time from when you go to work till you return. But child care and guard duty are two separate functions."

Good point. "My mother should be able to help. Especially if you go out, since that's when you'll need to be especially cautious. But…" Might as well give this a shot. "What I'd really like is for you to move in. Be there 24/7."

"I think she's safe enough with you on the premises," Patty advised.

Alec's pride urged him to agree with her, but this was no time for arrogance. "If they hire someone to kidnap my daughter, or if Sabrina shows up with Eduardo, I may not be able to handle it."

He noted the wry twist of her mouth. "You're asking me to move in with you?"

"You've seen Tatum's room. You'd have plenty of privacy." *Much as I might wish you were staying closer. Like, on the other side of my bed.*

"Down the hall," she said drily. "Practically in the next state, right?"

"In spite of what happened a few minutes ago, we have to do this for my daughter," Alec pressed. "Until after the party, anyway. I have a feeling that whatever Sabrina's up to, she'll pull it off by then or lose interest. That's only two days."

And two nights.

"Let me talk to Mike," Patty replied coolly. "I'll catch up with you at the condo."

"Thanks for considering it." Alec wished he could add some brilliant comment to press his case. None presented itself.

So he got in the SUV, took a few deep breaths as instructed, and started the engine.

MOVING IN WITH ALEC.

She couldn't view it in those terms, Patty reflected as her car followed the SUV along Safe Harbor Boulevard. This was all about Fiona's security.

On her hands-free phone, she explained the situation to Mike. "If he wants to hire a night guard, I can subcontract that," he replied. "You're not going to be much use while you're asleep."

"Agreed." She ought to feel relieved that she could stay home. It would be up to Alec whether he chose to hire additional protection at night. "I'll be more alert if I'm well rested, anyway."

"Exactly. In the meantime, I'll cover your other cases so you can spend your days and evenings with the Dennys. And, Patty?"

"Yes?"

"Since he hasn't told his ex about hiring a guard, I'm going to recommend we continue to keep her in the dark as long as possible." They'd decided that, given Sabrina's volatile moods, learning about Alec's security arrangements was as likely to intensify her anger as to dissuade her. "Posing as a nanny could give you a tactical advantage."

"Agreed."

With that decision made, Patty sketched in her findings on the runaway boy and promised to send her notes so Mike could take over. By that time, she'd arrived at the condo complex. Nothing unusual going on, a quick scan told her. No crazy ladies peering from the bushes, no commandos leaping from helicopters, no well-cloaked homeless person who might turn out to be a kidnapper for hire.

Instead, afternoon sunshine had broken through the over-cast morning, typical of May weather around here. Beyond the bluffs, sunlight sparkled off the ocean, while seabirds circled, mewing.

From the gated parking lot, Alec moved with contained purpose, body tight, mouth set in a firm line. If they were more than friends, more than business associates, they would lace their fingers together and hurry in side by side, awareness simmering between them.

And if you keep thinking this way, you'll fail him in the worst way possible.

"Mike's cleared my schedule to work double shifts for you through Sunday. Longer if you need me," she told him as they double-timed it along the walkway. "He can subcontract for a night guard if you like."

Alec's jaw clenched. "I'd rather have you."

"I'm not much use in my sleep. Besides, the police can be here in a few minutes." She worked more than enough night patrols in Safe Harbor to know how quickly they could arrive at a scene.

"It isn't the same as having you right there." He broke off. "But I understand. And no, I don't want a night guard. I'm trying to keep things as normal as possible for Fiona, although that seems to be getting harder and harder."

As they neared the stairwell, Patty watched for any movement. Nothing stirred. "Have you talked to your mother?"

"Yes. She's not exactly surprised. She figured Tatum would bolt sooner or later."

So had Patty, but she'd hoped the nanny would stay until after the party. This must be rough on the little girl. "Your ex doesn't seem to care how much disruption she causes for her daughter."

"This is the same woman who left a three-year-old alone in a car," he reminded her.

"I haven't forgotten."

Ahead, Patty saw the door to Alec's condo open slowly. Putting out an arm to halt him, she edged closer. Out rolled a suitcase, pushed over the sill by a running shoe. The crack in the door widened, and Tatum shouldered her way through, burdened by a backpack plus a laptop shoulder bag. To Patty, her skin looked even paler than usual, and she gave a start when she saw Alec.

"You're leaving already?" he asked.

"Got a flight in an hour from John Wayne." That was Orange County's airport, named for the famous local resident who, during his lifetime, had despised the noise from airplanes flying over his home.

"Who's watching Fiona?" he asked. Below, Patty saw a taxi approaching along the street.

"Your mother was resting, so she sent the housekeeper until you got here." Catching his frown, the nanny added, "It's okay. Rosita raised two kids of her own. She's teaching Fiona how to play a card game called *casita robada*. Kind of a go-fish type thing."

"I'm sorry you're leaving. Let me write you a check for whatever I owe you, plus your airfare."

"You can mail it to me. I left a note with my mother's address and the amount." Tugging her braid free of her shoulder strap, Tatum grabbed the suitcase. "I'm sorry to jump ship this way, but I can't take all the drama. I told Fiona I miss my family and that's why I'm leaving. I hope she'll be okay. She's a little sweetie."

"Why the rush? There's no immediate risk." Patty wondered if there was some clue she'd missed about the latest call.

"Sabrina has a mean streak. You never know what that kind

of person will do." Below, the cabbie honked and Tatum gave a pronounced start. How terrible it must be to go through life so easily frightened, Patty thought. "You will give me a good reference, won't you, Mr. Denny?" the nanny asked.

"Of course," he replied. "You've done a fine job."

"Take a course in self-defense," Patty advised the young woman. "Once you feel more confident in your abilities…"

"I'll feel more confident when I'm home." Below, the cab driver tapped his horn again. Over the portico railing, Tatum yelled, "Be right there!" To Alec and Patty, she said, "Got to go. Bye." Off she sped, wheeling the suitcase behind her.

"Are you sure Sabrina didn't say anything else?" Patty asked Alec.

"I told you everything I know." He held the door for her. Kind of a funny thing to do for the woman he'd hired to take out the opposition, Patty reflected, but she appreciated the gesture.

Inside, past the living room, Fiona and an older woman sat across from each other at the kitchen table, slapping down cards and giggling. "I win!" the little girl cried gleefully.

"You are smart girl." The thin lady, her graying hair pulled back in a bun, reached across to pat Fiona's hand. "First time you play, you win."

"You let me." The child grinned. "I can tell."

"*Very* smart girl." Rosita got to her feet. "Dr. Denny, no need to hurry home. I finish cleaning your mother's place and now is turn to clean yours, so no problem."

"Thank you for watching my daughter."

"Is fun for me."

Mike had run a check and found both Rosita's references from Houston and her credit rating excellent. While he hadn't been able to confirm that she was Marla's cousin, Patty already suspected that the old housekeeper's nieces weren't all related to her, either. An informal system of job-sharing probably worked to everyone's advantage, except possibly Darlene's. However, Rosita had made a good impression so far.

A light breeze rippled through the living room from the partly open balcony door. Patty strode over, and was glad to see it anchored by a floor lock, its four-inch gap wide enough for cool air to circulate but too narrow for anyone to sneak through.

"If you don't mind, Rosita, I'd rather you waited until later to clean," Alec said. "Patty and I have a few things to discuss with my daughter."

"I understand." The woman hesitated. "You will hire new nanny, *sí?*" What was she going to do? Patty wondered. Recommend some other "cousin"?

"For now, my mother and Patty will look after Fiona," Alec replied.

"Bueno." Rosita bobbed her head in accord. "Years ago, my daughter have a stalker. I chase him away with my broom. Give him one, two good whacks."

Patty couldn't help chuckling. "You may have missed your calling. You sound like a fierce protector."

"I do anything for my family," the housekeeper replied. "Now I work here, this is like my family."

Alec escorted her to the door. "While I appreciate your concern, remember that Patty and Mike are the experts. If there's any danger, they'll handle it."

"Sí, sí." With a little wave to Fiona, who was putting the cards into their box, Rosita departed.

Alec went to the table, where his daughter struggled to push the last card into the tight deck. "I can do that." Gently, he took over the task.

The little girl pressed her lips together. Her high spirits of a moment ago had vanished. "Why did Tatum leave?"

"She misses her family. She told you that, right?" Alec glanced at Patty as if for confirmation.

Patty might not have much experience with children, but she hadn't forgotten how, as a child, she'd hated being kept in the dark by social workers after her parents' arrest on drug charges. Being unable to get the facts had intensified her anxiety. What a relief it had been when Grandpa arrived and told the unvarnished truth, ugly as it was.

"Alec?" she said. "May I?"

She could tell he grasped what she was asking. "Do what you think is best."

Patty pulled up a chair at the table. "Tatum got a phone call that scared her."

"From Mommy?"

"Yes," Alec said. Patty was glad to see him taking his cue from her approach. "Mommy called Tatum a bad name."

Tears glistened in the little girl's eyes. "Will Mommy mess up my birthday?"

Patty longed to erase the child's pain. "I'm here to make sure that doesn't happen."

"Me, too." Quietly, Alec added, "Sabrina threw a tantrum last year. Really spoiled the occasion."

Fiona sniffled and gazed at him hopefully. "Is Patty going to stay with us?"

With a twinge, Patty saw why Alec wanted her here all the time: to reassure his daughter. But there were strong arguments against that. Above all, it would be hard to maintain a professional distance while wandering about in her pajamas. Even now, Patty would have to be diligent to ensure that her tenderness for these two and her anger toward Sabrina didn't interfere with her ability to protect them.

"I'll be here first thing in the morning, and I'll stay until your daddy's home at night," Patty said.

"Will you come to my party?" Fiona was hugging Hoppity.

"I wouldn't miss it!"

On the kitchen counter, the phone rang. All three of them gave a start. *We're as bad as Tatum,* Patty thought.

She walked over beside Alec. The readout showed a phone number with a Manhattan area code, but no name. "I don't recognize it," he said in a low voice.

"I'll get on the extension." She preferred to listen that way rather than using the speaker function, since the change in sound quality might tip off the caller. "Wait until you hear me clap, then pick up."

"Shouldn't we try to record it?"

"Under California law, you'd have to advise her first."

Alec shot Patty a look of frustration. "Never mind."

She reached the extension in the master bedroom on ring three. Clapped, and picked up just as Alec did. Tautly, she listened to his "Yes?"

"You left me a message to call." Impatience laced the female voice. "I already bought my plane ticket, so don't try to talk me out of coming for my daughter's birthday. Besides, as I mentioned, Eduardo has some business out there."

Apparently she was still in Manhattan. No guarantees about that, though.

"When do you arrive?" Alec asked.

"On Saturday, what do you think?" Sabrina snapped. Patty tried to reconcile that petulant voice with the stunning, doe-eyed woman she'd seen in Fiona's framed picture. Never trust a pretty package, Grandpa used to say. "You are giving her a party, aren't you? When is it and where?"

With obvious reluctance, he told her the time and place. "Where are you calling from?" Alec added. "I don't recognize the number."

"It's my new cell phone."

"What happened to the old one?"

"Why should you care?"

Fiona wandered in and Patty put a finger to her lips. When the child silently perched on the queen-size bed, Patty sat beside her and slid an arm around the little girl's waist. At this close range, Fiona could probably hear some of her mother's remarks, and Patty was ready to move away quickly if the situation deteriorated. But all things considered, she preferred openness.

"A woman called from your old cell phone and threatened Tatum," Alec said. "Was that you?"

"Did she say it was me?"

In conducting interrogations, Patty had learn that liars frequently answered a question with a question.

"She couldn't tell," Alec conceded.

"Well, my phone got stolen a few days ago, along with a few other things," Sabrina told him. "Including jewelry, but not the good stuff, because that's in a safe. We think the carpet cleaners took them, but of course they deny it."

"Why would the carpet cleaners threaten my nanny?" he demanded.

Hugging the bunny with one arm, Fiona nestled close. She seemed to be trying to bury her nose in Patty's side and the bunny's tummy at the same time, which kind of tickled.

"Maybe it was somebody's idea of a prank. Or Tatum imagined it. That girl hates me. I'm not fond of her, either."

Patty could almost hear Alec's teeth grinding as he answered, "She left."

"Really? Well, that's good news. Have you hired a replacement yet?"

"As a matter of fact, yes. You know, this whole situation is upsetting Fiona," Alec went on.

"Oh, pooh. She'll be fine," Sabrina retorted. "I'll see you Saturday." Without waiting for a goodbye, she cut off the call.

Mentally, Patty reviewed the conversation. The excuses

about the old cell phone raised a red flag. People with some-thing to hide played the maybe-this maybe-that game, seizing on a new explanation as soon as the old one fell short. Those who told the truth usually presented their story and stuck to it. On the other hand, she didn't see what Sabrina gained by making a threat from her old cell, then pretending it had been stolen.

Except to stir up a lot of trouble. Which seemed to be the woman's MO.

Patty rested her cheek on the little girl's head. "It's scary when grown-ups argue, isn't it?"

She felt the answering nod. "That's why you're here. To protect me," the child quavered.

"Exactly."

Even before Alec came in, even before she saw the tension in every fiber of his body, Patty knew she'd never be able to sleep well at home. She would worry about phone calls, about Fiona having nightmares, about Alec lying there keyed up, mentally fighting battles.

Battles that might turn out to be real. It was all too easy to underestimate danger and let your guard down. To overlook that one vulnerable moment when a hired kidnapper broke in and grabbed the little girl, or when Alec opened the door, expecting his mother, and found himself facing his bitter ex-wife with a container of battery acid or a gun in her hand.

Might as well move in. "I'll go home and pack," she told him. She'd figure out how to explain it to Mike later.

Chapter Twelve

"If you're a police officer, why don't you wear a uniform?" Fiona asked. With her three favorite stuffed animals arrayed around her on the bed, she was asking her umpteenth question of the evening. In addition to her usual reluctance to go to sleep, she was still excited about Patty's return at dinnertime with duffel bag in hand.

Patty seemed completely at home beside Fiona with her jean-clad legs stretched along the bed. But then, Alec mused, she had a gift for making herself at home wherever she was.

"I'm not a police officer anymore," Patty explained patiently, having gone over this point several times.

"But you're protecting me. Isn't that what police do?"

"Police work for the city. I'm a private detective. People can come and hire me. It's more personal." As Patty's gaze caught Alec's, a glow spread through him at this cozy scene. It seemed so natural, he had to remind himself that they'd come together only because of his ex-wife.

Earlier, when she'd agreed to spend the next few nights here for everyone's peace of mind, he'd felt a burst of exhilaration that had nothing to do with safety issues. Being around Patty simply felt right. After dinner, they'd made popcorn and all three of them had curled up on the couch to watch a favorite DVD, *Ghostbusters*. They'd chortled at the goofy antics, feigned terror at the funny-scary parts and shrieked with delight when the Stay Puft Marshmallow Man stalked the city streets.

For too long, Alec had missed that sense of abandon. Best of all, seeing the two adults acting silly had helped Fiona recover her high spirits.

"Does my daddy pay you?" Fiona was asking at the moment.

"Yes."

"I thought you were his friend."

"She earns her living as a detective. If I didn't pay her, she'd have to be off working somewhere else," Alec explained.

"Is that why she didn't visit us in Boston?" The little girl nuzzled her panda.

"Your daddy and I were friends growing up," Patty told her. "We stopped for a while, but now we're friends again." A mischievous glance slanted toward him. Friends. Yes. Was it possible, when this was over and she no longer worked for him, that she could still be part of his life?

"Why'd you stop? Did you fight?" Fiona asked, her expression troubled. With a pang, Alec realized she must be thinking about the way he and Sabrina had yelled at each other as their marriage had broken down. Although he'd tried to maintain composure in front of Fiona, sometimes he'd lost his temper. Despite his care not to use ugly terms, children picked up readily on an angry tone of voice.

"No, we didn't fight," Patty said.

"Then why...?"

"Sometimes circumstances, or other people, come between friends. It wasn't my fault and it wasn't your daddy's, either."

As a sleepy Fiona searched for more questions, guilt darkened Alec's mood. It was wrong to let Patty go on believing that his parents had forced them to split. Until now, he'd seen no reason to tell her the whole story. With her living under his roof, however, his continued silence made the lie seem far worse.

He wasn't a confused kid anymore. Whatever wild side she brought out in him he could deal with. Besides, he *liked* what she brought out in him.

After Fiona lost her struggle to keep her eyes open, he followed Patty into the kitchen. She rooted around into her duffel bag and took out a package of graham crackers, a bag of marshmallows and two chocolate bars.

Casting a glance toward the hallway, she explained, "I may not have much experience as a nanny but I doubt eating sweets at bedtime is good for kids, eh, doc?"

"It's not exactly healthy for grown-ups, either." When had he grown so prim and proper? Alec wondered, so he added, "But who cares?"

"Watching *Ghostbusters* always makes me hungry for s'mores. I brought this stuff along for the grown-ups." From a cabinet, she handed him a plate. "I'll show you how to make them."

"What makes you think I don't know?"

"Do you?"

Trust Patty to go right to the heart of the matter. "Only in the theoretical sense."

"I suspected as much. Watch and learn what you've been missing." On her plate, she slapped down a double-sectioned graham cracker and topped it with two marshmallows. Into the microwave they went for ten seconds, enough for them to puff to double their size.

Alec leaned against the counter. "Patty, there's something I've been meaning to tell you."

"If it has anything to do with the size of my butt, save it." She whisked out the plate. "Okay, now this part you have to do fast, before you lose the heat."

"I like the size of your butt."

"That's good. I may have to skip working out at the gym for this weekend, but I'll be back at it next week. So the butt, ample as it is, won't be growing." She slapped a chocolate bar atop the layer of marshmallows, then topped that with another graham cracker and pressed until the marshmallow oozed out the sides, its heat half melting the chocolate. "What was it you started to say?"

He took a deep breath. It hadn't been hard telling Bailey at the wedding reception, so why did he suddenly have to search for words? "Remember when we broke up?"

"I hope that's not a serious question."

"No, it isn't." *Just go for it.* "I didn't tell you the whole story."

She stopped with the gooey chocolate concoction halfway to her mouth. Alec had the uneasy impression that it took a lot to freeze Patty with a s'more inches from her lips. "Yeah?"

"My parents did pressure me pretty hard. They said if I didn't bring up my SAT scores, and lost out on scholarships, they weren't going to help pay the gap between my college savings and my expenses. That would have been a pretty big gap."

She set down the plate. "You said they threatened to cut you off entirely unless you dropped me. No college fund, no nothing."

"They didn't go that far," Alec admitted.

"Then why'd you dump me?"

"Because I kept getting into trouble around you. I figured sooner or later I was likely to screw something up that couldn't be fixed." That sounded lame, even to him.

"I didn't pour drinks down your throat the night before the SATs." She had an unusual air of stillness. He almost wished she'd show anger. Disgust. Whatever she was feeling.

Maybe it went too deep. The idea cut like a knife. Patty always seemed so resilient! "I know. I'm sorry."

"If you didn't think I was good enough for you—no, wait—if you decided I was the wrong girl for you, you should have told me." Patty folded her arms. "I wouldn't have shot you, although I did go out and shoot some clay pigeons in your honor."

"I'm sure they richly deserved it." He'd have enjoyed throwing the targets into the air and shooting alongside her. Except that hadn't been the idea, had it?

"Why'd you lie?" she pressed.

"Because I didn't trust myself," Alec said.

"You mean you didn't trust me." Her face was still unreadable.

"I didn't trust the part of myself that came out around you," Alec said. "Patty, at seventeen, I had this adolescent streak of rebellion, but our academic system doesn't grant any leeway. Everything's on the record. Everything counts. I was competing with people who never screwed up, who kept their noses to the grindstone. And I didn't hail from any special group that the powers-that-be make allowances for. No impoverished background, no physical handicaps to overcome. So I had to be perfect."

"Except to me." Pain shimmered in her eyes. A kind of pain he'd never seen in her before, not even then. Or perhaps he'd been too immature to recognize it.

"I didn't mean to be cruel. But I was, and I regret it. A lot." He squelched the urge to keep talking, to tell her he'd come clean because he didn't want half-truths and secrets to stand between them. He'd had no idea that the old wounds he was reopening had cut so deep.

She regarded him with no trace of the warmth they'd shared earlier. "It's good that you told me. Like turning on the lights so I can see things clearly."

How do I fix this? How do I make her smile again? No chance of that tonight, he feared. But…eventually?

He recognized now that his long silence had added weight to his deception. While he'd gone about his studies and married and had a child, Patty had had to cope with a broken heart. That was what he'd inflicted. Unwittingly. Stupidly. Selfishly. But throughout, she'd had the consolation that his parents had forced his hand.

Now he'd taken that away. She had every reason to think less of him. A lot less.

"Well." Patty glanced down at her plate. "Guess I'll eat this while I unpack." Slinging the duffel over her shoulder, she grabbed the snack and walked off.

At least she was heading for the hallway instead of the exit. Alec had to be grateful for that.

THIS ROOM WAS TOO SMALL. At the moment, the condo felt too small, as well, although it had more square footage than the house Patty was renting. In her current mood, the entire town of Safe Harbor might be too small.

As she unpacked, it took all her self-control not to slam the drawers or smack the hangers around in the closet. Alec had *chosen* to break up with her. She'd ached for him and longed for him and made a fool of herself in front of Grandpa. If Alec couldn't control his own choices and had to punish her for them, maybe the guy really was too weak for her.

That had been a dozen years ago. He'd faced up to it now. Couldn't he have broken it to her sooner? Or waited until she'd enjoyed her snack? It had gone cold. Just not the same. Tasted good, though. Chocolate, marshmallow…

It galled Patty to admit how much his lie had affected her. In her heart, she'd sheltered a tiny kernel of belief that at some level Alec had been just as devastated as she was by their breakup. Even though she'd accepted that he'd happily married a woman who pleased his parents, she'd compared other men to him and found them lacking. She'd wept at movies about lovers forced to part—okay, she'd jeered at them along with her guy friends, but there'd been the occasional traitorous tear in the corner of her eye.

If he'd told her the truth in high school, it would have knocked her flat. Opened a bleeding gash for everyone to see. But then she would have *healed*. Because she'd have seen that Grandpa was right and Alec didn't deserve her.

In fairness, she supposed his reasons for dumping her had been valid enough by his standards. He'd set the bar high in his career, and achieved it. You had to admire that. But…hey, weird thought. All this while she'd kept her distance from Darlene Denny who, it turned out, hadn't disliked her quite as intensely as she'd thought. Patty was tempted to march down there and apologize, except she couldn't figure out for what. The person who ought to apologize was Alec.

He had. But not enough. Twelve years shy of enough.

Well, she'd promised Fiona she'd stick around for the weekend, and she'd secured Mike's reluctant consent. He hadn't been keen on the idea, but she'd assured him Alec understood she couldn't stand guard duty in her sleep. So as long as she'd committed herself, she might as well stick it out and quit holding a pity party.

After licking the last of the chocolate off her fingers, Patty went to the bathroom to wash her hands. From the living room, she could hear the TV. It sounded like a documentary, some fellow with a British accent droning on about future technologies. These days, that meant about five minutes from now.

While washing, she started to hum "Twinkle Twinkle Little Star." Even after she stopped, the annoying melody kept playing through her head.

Back in her room, Patty pushed the tune aside and sat down

to take a hard look at Sabrina's latest actions and see if she could dope out any clues to what the woman might do next. In her laptop, she typed:

Calls and threatens nanny.

What had that accomplished? Tatum's departure might work to Sabrina's benefit if she intended to go back to court and claim Alec wasn't providing a stable environment. More likely, it showed pure meanness and a disregard for Fiona's feelings.

How sneaky, to keep the call so short that Tatum hadn't been able to make a positive voice ID. Still, Sabrina's usual tactic was to vent, not use restraint.

Could it be Eduardo's influence? He had to be a cold character, to abandon his wife and kids. Rich, successful, a smooth operator. Was this some kind of game to him? Or did he have more self-serving goals?

According to Mike's research, the Patron family owned a large food-packaging plant that exported many of its products. In addition, they'd acquired a small firm in the biotechnology field and were reputed to be investigating ways to expand its product line through research.

Mike had said he didn't see what Eduardo had to gain by antagonizing Alec. If anything, the lab director might prove a valuable connection to help identify growth areas in fertility treatment. This had become a major field in medicine, now that more women were waiting until their thirties, forties and sometimes even fifties to complete their families. And California, with its wide-open laws about fertility procedures, including in vitro, surrogacy and egg donation, was one of the centers.

None of this gave Eduardo a motive to tick off Alec.

Patty jotted another note:

Claims apartment break-in.

If that were true, there should be a police report. Mike could check it out. Still, a real burglary wouldn't preclude the possibility that Sabrina had lied about the phone's being stolen.

Note number three:

She and fiancé to fly here Saturday.

Sabrina was entitled to a supervised visit on her daughter's birthday, so that didn't violate the custody agreement. Still, it meant matters were likely to come to a head quickly.

Patty summarized her observations on these new developments and emailed the report to Mike. He could confirm with Manhattan police whether there'd been a break-in, and might even be able to determine exactly when Sabrina was scheduled to arrive. Patty sent a copy to Alec, with a matter-of-fact recommendation that he keep the police updated about his ex-wife's activities.

Have I overlooked anything? She was glad Mike would be reviewing her observations, because regardless of her opinion of Alec, she'd never let anything hurt his little girl.

Or him.

No matter how well they prepared, though, Patty had to be ready to adjust to events on the fly. Especially on Saturday at the party. There'd be a lot of people coming and going: children, parents, pizza deliverers. Mike planned to restrict access to a single door, while Patty would stick close to Fiona, but this wasn't a presidential visit complete with Secret Service. Had there been a better-defined threat, or indications that Sabrina had hired a professional, Mike would have recommended augmenting the staff. Instead, there'd be just the two of them.

Plus Alec, of course. Patty's gut squeezed as she remembered the affection in his dark eyes during Fiona's bedtime session. With the three of them gathered together, they'd almost felt like a family.

For a moment, she'd actually wanted that. The longing had sprung up unbidden, after years of believing she wasn't suited for domestic life. A husband, children. She'd never believed she could make a go of that stuff, not with her background.

Or had the prospect seemed empty because no man could compare to the idealized Alec of her memory? The fellow who'd been nothing but a liar, after all.

Perhaps now she could get past that. Now that she was free of her illusions.

Wishing she hadn't wasted the ingredients for a second s'more on her deceitful old friend, Patty poked through the list of movies on her laptop and picked one of the *Rocky* films. Didn't matter which one, as long as it involved punching somebody's lights out and winning big.

Chapter Thirteen

Alec had hoped that a good night's sleep would soften Patty's reaction to his confession. He, for one, barely slept, and awoke with the sense that someone had sandpapered his skin.

In the kitchen, he found her already showered and dressed in jeans and a blouse, serving Fiona cereal at the counter. They'd forgotten to brush out the little girl's hair last night, Alec noted. Light brown wisps had pulled free from the braid, along with several longer strands.

After kissing his daughter, he turned to Patty. "Good morning." He watched her reaction, hoping for some hint of encouragement.

"Morning." The word came out crisp and impersonal. "Did you receive my report? I emailed it last night."

"I did," he confirmed, and popped two slices of bread in the toaster. "Good job."

Fiona jostled her bowl, sending milk spattering onto the counter. "Oops." Her eyes rounded guiltily.

Alec was about to reach for the sponge when Patty tore off a paper towel and handed it to her charge. Then she stood there with arms folded.

"You want me to clean it up?" Fiona asked in surprise.

"You made the mess. You're old enough to clean it up."

"Okay." Solemnly, the little girl wadded the towel and mopped the table clean.

Alec was impressed. "You make a good nanny. If a bit unconventional."

"Kids need to own their lives. That means making decisions and dealing with the consequences. Appropriately for their age," Patty added. "That's what I learned being raised by a military man."

"I always figured the Sergeant would have liked me better if I'd saluted." Alec hadn't exactly felt antagonism from Patty's grandfather, but the man had displayed about as much welcome as he would to a broken axle at his garage. "Aren't you eating?"

"Already had a certain item you didn't fix for yourself last night." She refrained from mentioning in front of Fiona that she'd eaten a chocolate bar, marshmallows and graham crackers for breakfast. Candy bars morning, night and no doubt noon, as well.

"There is something to be said for nutrition," he observed drily as he poured himself a cup of coffee. "By the way, thanks for making this."

"You're low on filters."

He nearly told her that grocery shopping was her job, when he remembered it wasn't. "I'll pick some up. So, what're you planning to do today?"

"I plan to keep Fiona safe," Patty said.

"Don't you have some activities in mind?"

"I'm not actually a nanny," she reminded him.

"You could fix my hair," Fiona chirped.

"What's wrong with it?" Patty glanced at the girl's braid. "Yeah, looks a little messy. We should chop that off."

"Yay!"

Alec stopped in the middle of buttering his toast. "You *like* the idea?"

"I hate braiding my hair," Fiona informed him. "I want to look like Patty."

This could be a problem, Alec reflected as he weighed how to respond. Not the hair per se, but this eagerness to model herself after someone who didn't intend to stay around very long. With Tatum's abdication, Fiona was seizing on the nearest mother substitute—aside from Darlene, since apparently grandmothers didn't hold quite the same appeal. What was going to happen when guard duty ended?

He knew what he'd like to see happen. But after last night, any renewed friendship seemed a distant possibility.

"Well?" demanded Fiona.

He hadn't meant to keep her waiting. "You can have your hair done as a birthday treat. Patty, would you mind setting that up?"

"I don't advise visiting a salon." Her voice drifted back from where she'd stuck her head in the fridge. "Too many people, too hard to control the situation. Are you saving this pudding for anything?"

"You can't eat pudding for breakfast!" Fiona cried.

"How about for a snack?"

"If you don't eat right, you'll get sick." His daughter's mouth pursed. "Your bones will crumble. Your hair will fall out and you'll be bald."

"Where did you hear that?" Alec was amazed at the things that came out of this little girl's mouth.

"Tatum told me." Earnestly, she added, "Well, I made up some of it. But it's probably true."

From the depths of the refrigerator, Patty emerged wielding a stick of celery. "If I eat this, will my bones get strong?"

Fiona nodded.

"Okay, then." She crunched into it. "Mmm. I feel tougher already."

Alec refrained from pointing out that celery wasn't a major source of calcium. Anything that persuaded Patty to eat a vegetable ought to be encouraged.

He wished he could hang around to see who ended up nannying whom, but he had work to do. "Be careful. Call me if you need me." He took his dishes to the sink, kissed his daughter and left, taking care to bolt the door.

WHAT WAS SHE GOING TO DO for an entire day with a little girl? The kid wasn't old enough to go to the shooting range or, from a practical standpoint, to play pool, given that she'd have to stand on a chair to reach the table. Besides, you didn't take a client home with you.

The hair-salon idea was beginning to sound tempting. Especially after Patty learned from Mike that there *had* been a police report filed about the break-in at Eduardo's penthouse. This meant Sabrina truly might not have made the last threatening call.

Of course, someone had, and Patty refused to write it off as a prank. Which left her with an increasingly restive four-going-on-five-year-old and the challenge of protecting without smothering her.

Patty mulled the options. Being in public exposed them to attack. Staying put made them predictable as targets. Then there remained the possibility that no one was after Fiona and they'd self-destruct from sheer boredom. Besides, if Darlene could accompany them, to help stand watch, they should be safe enough at a beauty parlor.

After making sure Darlene was home, they went downstairs, where they found the smaller condo stuffed with packages of party decorations and medical supplies. Rosita, who'd stopped by the supermarket on her way to work, was unloading groceries in the kitchen.

"I'd love to go to the hairdresser with you, but my ankle's hurting again," Darlene said wistfully from the couch, where she sat distributing small toys among goody bags for tomorrow's little guests. "I don't think of myself as old, but my body doesn't heal like it used to."

"She should eat more celery, right, Fi?" Patty asked.

"And soup," the little girl said, hugging her grandmother. "Salad's good, except for the bitter stuff."

"I hate the bitter stuff, too." Her grandmother smiled. "We should all go out for lunch to a place with a salad bar. Not today, though, and obviously tomorrow's taken. How about Sunday? I'd like to get to know you better," she said to Patty.

"Sure. Thanks." Patty wasn't sure who or what to credit for this détente with Darlene, but she was grateful for it. She'd spent too many years blaming the older woman for something that hadn't been her fault.

"Now I have a suggestion about—

"Yes, Rosita?" Darlene glanced at the housekeeper, who stood with a couple of cake-mix boxes in hand.

"Fiona needs to pick which I bake tomorrow." To Patty, the woman explained, "Mrs. Denny ask me to buy two flavors."

"Wow! Chocolate *and* lemon!" The little girl ran to examine the packages. "What kind of frosting?"

"Come and I'll show you." The gray-haired woman led her to the open kitchen, far enough away to be nearly out of earshot.

"Rosita's a vast improvement over Marla's other relatives," Darlene said quietly. "She's even agreed to come in tomorrow morning to bake and decorate."

Good, because when it came to ovens, Patty was still trying to figure out why they bothered with that confusing preheat option. "Great. You mentioned a suggestion?"

"Kate Franco used to be my hairdresser over at the My Fair Lady Salon. I miss her, now that she's married to that lawyer and staying home with the baby." The older woman's birdlike hands darted from one sack to the other, topping them off with miniature cars. "In fact, her son Brady is coming to the party tomorrow. I'll bet she'd cut Fiona's hair at her house, if I asked. How about it?"

Patty liked Leo's sister-in-law, and the outing sounded like a good compromise from a safety versus going-out-of-our-minds standpoint. "Super. It has my stamp of approval."

Darlene folded her hands in her lap. "Before I call, there's something else I'd like to say while Fiona's out of the room."

"Uh, sure." Patty eyed her warily. When people requested a private conversation, that usually meant they had something to unload.

"I used to be a terrible snob." Since Darlene made it a simple declaration of fact, Patty didn't argue. "You may recall that I was a college English instructor, and Howard was an anesthesiologist. We expected our son to be a high-achiever, academically speaking. When he brought you around, well, you didn't fit into our expectations."

Patty didn't take offense at this obvious truth. "Yeah, I wasn't exactly a parent's dream come true."

"Some parents ought to take a closer look at their dreams." The older woman leaned forward and patted Patty's hand. "Sabrina impressed us. She was glamorous, educated, sophisticated and a complete poison pill. We should have appreciated what a gem you were. A diamond in the rough. Patty, I'm sorry I underestimated you."

"That's okay." This honest disclosure called for a frank response. "I wasn't crazy about you, either."

Darlene burst out laughing. "You're priceless!"

"I like you better now," Patty admitted.

"I like you better now, too, and I'm grateful that you're available to watch over my granddaughter." She picked up the phone. "On that note, I'll call Kate."

Tony's wife readily agreed, and a few minutes later, Patty found herself piloting her car, with a buoyant Fiona alongside her, toward the Francos' bluffside home. While the little girl chattered about how she'd persuaded Rosita to bake cupcakes in both flavors, Patty watched the mirrors and kept an eye out for anyone following them or lurking ahead, ready to box them in. Traffic proved light, no one blocked their path, and they pulled safely into the drive of the Mediterranean-style home.

What a gorgeous place, Patty reflected as the short, radiant Mrs. Franco greeted them and led them through the house. Sunlight bathed the large rooms and stylish but comfortable furniture. Patty especially liked the curving front staircase and large bay window in the sunroom, but the best part was the covered patio and reflecting pool landscaped with rocks and ferns. An outdoor kitchen made the backyard absolutely perfect.

Kate indicated a chair she'd prepared with extra cushions, beside a table where she'd placed a plastic hairstyling cape and a set of scissors and hair clippers. "There's hardly any breeze today, so I thought it would be fun to sit outside. It's easier to clean up the hair, too," she said as she transferred her six-month-old daughter from her hip into a playpen.

Fiona climbed onto the cushions. "Where's Brady?"

"In kindergarten until noon. He'll be sorry he missed seeing you, Fiona. He can hardly wait till your party. What fun, to bring his favorite stuffed animals!" Kate covered her in the cape and fastened the Velcro at the back.

"Should be quite a kick. 'Scuse me a minute. Doing my guard duty." Patty had heard Darlene on the phone, explaining about Sabrina and the precautions they were taking. Besides, while it might be easy to pretend to strangers that Patty was a nanny, Kate knew all about her background.

So, while her hostess set to work on Fiona's hair, she paced around the yard. Just like at the condo development, the bluff made the place hard to access from behind. At either side, bushes and ferns obscured the fences. Peering through them, she took in the well-kept yards of the neighbors. No one stirring at the moment.

Patty returned to find Kate brushing out the little girl's hair. "A short bob would be easy to maintain," the hairdresser advised.

"I want to look like Patty." Fiona indicated Patty's chin-length cut.

"Her hair's straight. Yours has more curl, so they wouldn't look the same," Kate pointed out. "I've got another idea. Why don't I give you both short haircuts?"

Patty thought this over for about ten seconds. She never changed her hairstyle because she had no idea what to change it to, but here she had an expert volunteering. "Whatever you think will look good. I don't mind if it's prettier on Fiona than on me."

"Okay with you?" Kate asked Fiona.

"Yeah!"

As Kate gently sliced away Fiona's long hair, Patty couldn't help contrasting this luxurious home with the small, cozy cottage where Kate had previously lived. Patty and Leo had visited it once to write up a report about a troubled teenage girl Kate had been helping.

"A person could sure get used to a place like this," Patty said. "I mean, maybe not me personally, but it's fun to visit."

"I still feel a little like an imposter. Tony and I have been married only for three months, you know." Kate murmured a few complimentary words to Fiona before picking up the subject again. "After my first husband died, Brady and I got by on a very tight budget. When I agreed to be a surrogate mom, and Esther brought me here to help her plan the nursery, it was like visiting an alien dimension."

Patty had heard the story from Leo, complete with sarcastic commentary about his brother's self-centered first wife. Ambitious and hard-driven, Esther had responded to her infertility by hiring another woman to bear their child—actually, Tony and Kate's, since Esther had suffered ovarian failure. All very well, except that partway through the pregnancy, Esther had decided to accept a prestigious job offer in Washington, D.C., abandoning her husband and their baby-to-be for the glamorous social life of a single woman on the rise.

"Leo admired you for refusing to live with Tony while he was still going through the divorce," Patty recalled.

"What kind of example would that have set for Brady if I'd moved in with a married man?" Kate moved around the chair, snipping carefully. "When Tony offered to be my birthing partner, I never imagined we'd fall in love. But sometimes wonderful things happen."

"Yeah, occasionally." Patty wasn't optimistic about her own chances in the romance department, but no sense burdening Kate with that. "So did you always plan to be a mom?"

"Always."

"Guess a person has to be born with that," she mused.

"You'd be a good mother, Patty." Kate kept her gaze on the little girl, checking the length of her newly cut bangs.

"I doubt it."

"You don't like kids?" Fiona asked in dismay.

Patty had forgotten the child was drinking in every word. "I like *you*. But I'm not good at mommy stuff. Never even played with dolls, unless you count action figures."

"You thought of the teddy-bear clinic!" her charge retorted.

"Your grandmother and Rosita are organizing it, not me," Patty pointed out.

"You're a good nanny." The girl seemed determined to win this argument.

"I'm your bodyguard. I'm here to protect you."

The little girl's mouth trembled. "That's all?"

Wasn't that enough? Patty supposed not. "Hey, you're more than a job to me. You're my friend." An unfamiliar impulse seized her, to give Fiona a reassuring hug. Not practical, though, what with the scissors whipping about.

"Why don't you want to be a mommy?" the girl persisted.

"For starters, I don't cook, except for spaghetti and omelets." Patty wished Fiona would stop looking so crushed. "Whenever I try to do girlie stuff, I screw it up. Once I read in a magazine that giving your hair a vinegar rinse made it shine. I didn't realize you had to wash it out, and went around all day smelling like a salad."

A chuckle broke the tension. "Did anybody try to eat you?"

"Luckily, no."

Kate gave the bangs one last snip and held up a mirror. The little girl turned this way and that to study the new style. "It's so short."

"It's adorable, you little pixie," Patty said. "I can't wait to get mine."

Fiona's smile could have lit up the universe. When Patty lifted her off the chair, the girl clung to her for a moment before alighting on the ground.

Holding her felt wonderful.

How unfair that the child had a lousy mother, and now she'd lost Tatum, too, Patty reflected as she removed the cushions and sat down. Alec was a great dad, but Fi needed a mommy-type person, too. Someone to love her. Someone to help her grow up and learn to dance and put on makeup and knock boys down if they got rough, and shoot clay pigeons when they left.

In the playpen, baby Tara waved a rattle and declared, "Ba ba ba."

Fiona plopped down on the ground, nose to nose with the infant. "I like babies. Is it okay if I want to be a mommy someday?"

"Absolutely." *It's not as if you have to reshape yourself in my image*, Patty thought. But how touching that the little girl valued her opinion.

Kate set to combing Patty's hair, and kept up a running stream of commentary to Fiona about the infant's development. As she listened, Patty sneaked glances at the two young ones. How would it feel to have tykes like these who depended on her, loved her, belonged to her? Plus a husband who kept the bed warm and shared the events of the day with her. A guy like Alec.

She'd enjoyed bustling around him at breakfast, inhaling his aftershave lotion, noting the sophisticated weave of his jacket. Touchable. Sexy. Too bad they belonged in different worlds. Except so had Kate and Tony, until they'd fallen in love.

Now stop that. Patty had better not be turning into one of those weak women Grandpa had deplored. Moping around, fantasizing, being ruled by emotions instead of good judgment and common sense.

"What do you think?"

Kate's question roused Patty from her reflections. To her amazement, she discovered that she'd daydreamed right through her haircut.

The hand mirror revealed a couple of startling facts. For one thing, she had a forehead, visible now that her thick bangs had been trimmed to wisps. For another, she had ears. Kind of cool to see them standing there proudly, not peeking shyly through the hair. She might even hang earrings off them once in a while. "Great job."

"We're twins." Fi watched her hopefully.

Patty removed the protective cape and did what she'd been longing to do: she grabbed the little girl, whirled her around and blew raspberries against her neck, making funny noises and raising delighted giggles. "We sure are! You're such a sweetheart." Now, where had that endearment come from? "Thank you, Kate."

"My pleasure." Their hostess lifted her baby from the pen. "I'll clean later. Right now I've got to collect Brady and take him to the hospital."

"Brady's sick?" Fiona asked worriedly.

"Oh, no, we're going to visit my sister Mary Beth. She just had a baby. It's her third child but first girl. We're all thrilled."

"Congrats." Patty wished her brother or sister would get married and produce a kid. The whole family was a real no-show in that regard. So far, anyway. "Oh, hey, Fi, aren't you going to take your braid home with you? Hang it on the wall or something?"

"Yeah!"

Patty rummaged in her purse and found a plastic bag. She always carried a few for evidence or anything else useful she might stumble across.

"And you said you aren't domestic." Kate escorted them through the house again. "I completely forgot about giving her the braid."

"That isn't domestic. It just struck me as a good idea." She held up a hand to stop their hostess from exiting first. No matter how safe the neighborhood appeared, Patty didn't believe in taking chances.

She moved to the front window to survey the street. All

appeared quiet, but Patty went out first. Nothing moved, and after a quick check around, she gave the all clear.

"Can I have ice cream for lunch?" Fiona asked as they said goodbye and went to the car.

"Not until you've eaten something healthy. How about a pickle-and-egg sandwich?"

"Ooh, yuck!"

Patty agreed. "I just made that up to be silly. How about a bacon-lettuce-and-tomato sandwich?" She'd seen the makings in the fridge.

"Hurray! Those are scrummy."

Patty wasn't sure how to fix a BLT, but she could find instructions on the internet. This domesticity business wasn't so hard, after all.

Chapter Fourteen

On Saturday morning, Alec helped his mother and Rosita festoon the clubhouse with hospital-themed decorations, including an eye chart and tables with signs such as Admissions, Diagnosis and Blood Pressure. Patty and Fiona sat on chairs blowing up balloons, a number of which escaped and scooted through the air with raucous noises that sent his daughter into fits of giggles.

He'd been startled to see the pair sporting look-alike haircuts last night when he'd arrived home for dinner. He couldn't stop peering from one to the other, admiring how much more freely Fiona moved her head without the restraining braid, and how artfully the style framed Patty's face, emphasizing her large gray eyes and sensual mouth.

Despite the similar cuts, there wasn't much physical resemblance between his fierce, brown-haired daughter and the confident blonde woman. But they seemed closer, making little jokes and teasing each other. Obviously, they'd had fun that day.

Most importantly, Fiona was safe. And that was what he and Patty both needed to focus on, today in particular. Although they still didn't know exactly when Sabrina would arrive, they couldn't legally stop her from paying a visit, supervised by Alec, of course. As for snatching their daughter, she hadn't repeated the threat, which hadn't been specific enough for the police to take action.

No matter how powerfully old embers sizzled, he should never have distracted Patty from her mission by bringing up the past, Alec reflected as he set his wrapped gifts on a table. Fiona's well-being was the only thing that mattered.

Mike Aaron arrived at 10:00 a.m., an hour before the party's scheduled start, and closed off the clubhouse's side door. "From now on, I monitor everyone who enters." The sandy-haired giant wielded his clipboard as if prepared to deflect bullets with it. "Any word from the ex?"

"Nada." Alec gave a start as his phone played the opening notes of Beethoven's Fifth Symphony.

"Might be her now."

"No, it's my boss." Wondering why Owen Tartikoff would be calling on a Saturday, Alec moved to a quiet corner.

"Alec. You at the lab?" As usual, the world-renowned fertility specialist skipped ordinary courtesies.

"Not this morning." Whatever question Owen had, Alec hoped answering it wouldn't require a trip to the office.

"Got a request from a former colleague, Dr. Laura Giovanni. She's a fertility specialist in Buenos Aires who's presenting a paper at the ISERF meeting next fall." That would be the annual conference of the International Society of Embryology and Reproductive Fertility, to be held in L.A. in October. Owen was scheduled to be the keynote speaker. "A member of her clinic's board of directors is visiting your area today and wants to see the facilities. I said you'd be happy to show him around."

Alec didn't know which to address first, an uneasy feeling about this director or the fact that he wasn't available to play tour guide. He decided on the latter. "Any chance he's staying over the weekend? I'm tied up today on personal business."

"The man owns a biotech company. Laura says he may be

interested in sponsoring research. What exactly is important enough for you to blow him off?" Owen spoke with the all-too-familiar sardonic tone that he splashed like acid over nurses and residents.

But Alec was neither of those. "It's my daughter's birthday party." He didn't bother to say how much this meant to Fiona, since that wouldn't help his case. Owen's interest in children dwindled to zero once they passed the embryo stage. "What's this fellow's name, anyway?"

Paper rustled in the background. "Edward something."

"Eduardo Patron?"

"You've heard of him?" A rare note of surprise colored the question. Owen wasn't used to being caught off guard.

"Mr. Patron is expected to attend the birthday party, since he's engaged to my ex-wife." Alec enjoyed being one step ahead of his boss for a change. "Did he request the tour with me specifically?"

"I have no idea. You think he's playing some kind of game?"

"It's possible." Sabrina's threats and the rest of the messy situation were none of Owen's business.

The doctor made a harrumphing noise. "I don't believe Laura would be a party to any nonsense. We went to Harvard Med School together and she's a straight shooter. As far as I'm concerned, the request is legitimate."

Alec stood his ground. "I'm sure he'll understand why I'm not available today. I'll be happy to take him around tomorrow. Even though it happens to be a Sunday." He could wield a touch of testiness himself.

Across three thousand miles, he visualized Owen finger-combing his bristly dark auburn hair as he reviewed this declaration. As always, a decision came swiftly. "Since you'll be seeing Mr. Patron today, you can work out the details with him. I'll email Laura and let her know."

"Great."

Click. No sign-off, but that was fine. When confronted in a reasonable fashion, Owen did occasionally back down. Alec believed his ability to get along with the notoriously abrasive man owed a lot to his refusal to be bullied.

Now, what kind of maneuver was Eduardo Patron trying to pull, and what did it mean for Fiona's safety? With the momentary sense of triumph fading, Alec went to fill in his security detail.

PATTY HAD GIVEN UP her teddy bear when she was eight. Grandpa hadn't stated any objection to Mr. Pooh when she and Drew had moved to Safe Harbor, but she'd registered the disapproving lift of the eyebrow whenever he saw her hugging the raggedy toy. After a while, she'd consigned Mr. Pooh to a bottom drawer, and eventually donated him as a dart target at a junior high game night. It had seemed a brave end for the warrior bear she imagined him to be.

Displays of stuffed animals still had the power to halt her in her tracks wherever she ran across them. At Christmas, she loved buying an armful to donate to the Toys for Tots collection at the police station.

Being surrounded by the little figures was sheer bliss. Not to mention the sweet innocence of the children as they raced from station to station, thrusting out their bears and bunnies and cartoon figures to be measured, weighed, bandaged and stitched. It took all Patty's concentration to stay alert for danger as she stuck close to Fiona.

Around her, everyone seemed merry and relaxed. Alec had explained Mike's presence by telling the parents about his ex-wife's tendency to create scenes. Other than that, Mike had advised against issuing a warning because the threat was so vague.

"Aren't they darling?" cooed Bailey, wearing her nurse's

uniform as she stood at the eye chart. "Okay, what's this line?"

"A-B-C-D-E-F-G." A small girl holding a large Mickey Mouse read off the letters in a squeaky voice.

"Perfect vision—twenty-twenty," the nurse declared.

"Can he have a pair of glasses, anyway?" The child pointed to a display of toy glasses frames.

"You bet." Bailey twisted a pair to fit over the big round ears. Neither Mickey nor his owner seemed to mind that they settled well above eye level.

"This is a great idea." Hospital childbirth instructor Tina Torres beamed at Patty, who realized the girl must have been her daughter. "The kids are learning not to be afraid of doctors."

"It's the best party I ever had," announced Fiona, hugging Hoppity.

"It's the best party anybody ever had," Patty corrected.

"Yeah!"

By twelve-thirty, all the stuffed animals had completed their physicals. Right on time, the pizza appeared. The half-dozen guests and their parents helped clear the tables for eating, while Bailey and Darlene served punch. Rosita had left before the guests arrived, tired from an early-morning shift spent baking and frosting enough cupcakes for a party twice this size.

Still no sign of Sabrina. "I'm sure she'll be here," observed Alec, putting away his wallet after paying for the pizza. "Eduardo went to a lot of trouble to try to draw me away." That was what they'd surmised to be the purpose of his request to tour the lab. "Maybe their flight was delayed."

Not likely, in Patty's opinion, since May was generally a fair weather month all across the country. "Let's hope."

She grabbed a slice of pizza and ate standing up, watching for trouble. Nothing materialized before the serving of the brown and yellow cupcakes, one of which bristled with five candles. As Darlene lit them, Alec leaned over his daughter. "Make a wish, sweetheart, and don't—"

"I want Patty to be my mommy."

"—tell anybody," he finished wryly.

"Oh, that's just an old superstition," Darlene said. "Blow 'em out, and more power to you."

A quiver ran through Patty, pleasure mixed with longing and bittersweet regret that Fiona's wish had no chance of coming true. Once the immediate danger was past, she and Alec would go their separate ways. Twelve years ago, he'd known in his gut that they didn't belong together, and at some level, maybe she'd known it, too.

She certainly did now.

Fiona screwed up her face and blew so hard one of the candles fell over. The flame extinguished itself, so no harm was done.

"Yay!" the kids yelled, mostly because this meant they could now bite into their own cupcakes.

"If I'd known being around kids meant eating all this good stuff, I'd have done more babysitting," Patty told Alec.

"Lemon or chocolate?" He held out a serving platter. "Don't tell me. Both."

"Not on duty. Got to keep one hand free." She started with chocolate.

After cupcakes and a lot of hand and face scrubbing with sterile wipes left over from the bear clinic, it was time to open gifts. Fiona took a seat surrounded by friends and a pile of packages.

Darlene handed her the gifts from the other children first. Gleefully, Fiona opened them to reveal games, DVDs, books, dolls and a fluffy bear. As she'd been instructed, she thanked each child and proclaimed the gifts just what she wanted.

"Don't ever say, 'Oh, I already have that,' or 'I don't like

that.' You wouldn't be happy if someone said that to you,'
Patty had warned earlier. "Besides, you can always exchange
things later."

Fiona had finished tearing through the first batch of gifts
when Mike signaled Alec. "They're here," he stated in a neutral tone. "Coming through the gate."

Through an expanse of glass, Patty spotted a model-thin
woman and a tall, distinguished-looking man, both far too
well dressed for a children's party. They stopped partway
along the walk, and the man took something from a shoulder
bag.

What was he doing? And why was he wielding a lighter?

A sharp series of *pop pop pops* sent Patty's heart slamming
into her throat. "Everybody down!"

Adults and children hit the floor. Outside, Patty saw a flash
of light. As arranged, Alec dialed 911, Mike drew his gun
and took cover in the doorway, and she threw her body over
Fiona's.

Whatever might happen, Patty was ready.

Chapter Fifteen

The entire room seemed to hold its breath. "All of you, please stay put." Mike stepped cautiously outside.

"You, too!" Patty called to Darlene, who'd stood up and was edging toward a window.

"It sounds like…" The older woman peered out. "Oh, for heaven's sake, they brought sparklers and party poppers."

With his phone in one hand, still apparently connected to the dispatcher, Alec pulled his mother gently but firmly away. "If you'd been mistaken, you could have been hit by flying glass." His worried gaze traveled to his daughter. "Everybody okay?"

"We're fine. People, please remain where you are in case this is a distraction." After murmuring reassurances to Fiona, Patty stood and surveyed the clubhouse to make sure no one had opened a side door or was behaving suspiciously. Everything appeared normal. A couple of parents had even started joking with the kids, as if this was a game, and a little girl scrambled to her feet.

"Down, please." Patty gestured until the child obeyed. "Everybody, treat this like an earthquake drill." In California, schools and entire towns held drills to prepare for quakes, ranging from duck-under-your-desk exercises to large scale run-throughs that tested hospital, fire department and police readiness. "Remember what Mike said. Nobody moves until we get the all clear."

"I had no idea nannies took safety this seriously," said one of the mothers. "Do they train you for this?"

"You bet."

"Is it going to be okay?" Fiona's words came out muffled because she had her nose buried in the bunny's fur.

"Sure. It's just your mom." Patty's heart ached for the little girl, who couldn't even enjoy her birthday party in peace, let alone count on her mother for support.

The child peeked up at her. "Can I open the rest of my presents now?"

"Later, little one." Patty continued to observe their surroundings for anything amiss. Outside, Mike had engaged the couple in conversation.

"But—"

"They won't sprout legs and trot off. I promise." Patty was glad to see an answering smile. She'd have liked to ease the tension even more, but not yet.

On the phone, Alec was explaining to the dispatcher that the explosions appeared to be harmless. "We'd appreciate having a patrol car stop by, but at this point it doesn't look like an emergency."

On the walkway, the tall woman tossed back her mane of dark hair impatiently. The suave fellow at her side, his pencil-thin mustache and gray-tinged black hair giving him a sophisticated air, spoke courteously to Mike.

Finally her boss signaled her, and Patty gave everyone the okay to get up. "That's just like Sabrina," Darlene grumbled. "She can't stand not being the center of attention."

"Those people certainly know how to make an entrance." Bailey brushed off her knees.

"Are you all right?" Patty asked Alec as he ended his call.

"Just seriously annoyed." He reached down to hug his daughter. "Sorry for the scare."

"That's okay, Daddy." Her little arms wound around him. The expression on her face was utterly trusting, and so achingly sweet, it was all Patty could do to tear her eyes away.

When Alec released Fiona, his hand brushed Patty's and he gave her a short, intense look. Something she didn't fully understand passed between them—partly a shared sense that they'd both been ready to risk their lives, but something else, too. A kind of belonging that ran so deep it almost scared her.

"I guess I'd better go invite them in," Alec muttered. "Fiona, you'll be fine with Patty."

"I know." She took Patty's hand and gripped it tight.

Outside, Eduardo was showing Mike a handful of fireworks that appeared from a distance to be harmless sparklers and noisemakers. All the same, they could burn a child's skin or cause serious eye damage.

"What a bad idea. Don't they realize how young these children are?" Tina complained as she and the other guests gathered around the refreshment table. A second helping of cupcakes seemed to soothe everyone's nerves.

Fiona stuck close to Patty. She didn't seem eager to greet her mother, and no wonder, Patty reflected, scrutinizing the new arrival through the glass. Sabrina Denny had an intimidating air, like a Thoroughbred horse ready to trample any hapless critter that skittered across her path.

It wasn't Patty's job to judge. She was here to protect the child and, secondarily, everyone else at the party.

Besides, Alec had once fallen in love with this woman, and she'd given birth to this precious little girl. There must be something worthwhile about her.

FROM THE TIME he was seventeen and made the decision to put his future ahead of his heart, Alec had embraced being an adult. He'd shouldered every responsibility that had come along, without question. But right now he wished he could act like a kid, tell his self-centered ex-wife where to get off, and send these intruders packing.

When the noisemakers had gone off, he'd felt a jolt of adrenaline and a pang of dread, not for himself but for Fiona. For an instant, he'd feared that all his efforts had been useless to protect the person he loved most in the world.

Then he'd seen Patty, fiercely protective and balanced, ready, trained. His first impulse had been to leap to his daughter's defense, but he'd been assigned a vital role, calling the police. And he'd been able to rely on Patty to be there, not only standing guard but also comforting Fiona.

She'd done her part. Now he had to paste a smile on his face and move forward to murmur a polite greeting to the woman he wished he never had to see again. And shake hands with a man who might turn out to be his worst enemy.

"Dr. Denny!" Eduardo gripped his hand eagerly. "I am very pleased to meet you."

"Mr. Patron. Welcome to Safe Harbor." Alec was glad for Mike's looming presence, because he didn't trust this fellow despite his friendliness. "I understand you're interested in seeing the lab. Will tomorrow be soon enough?"

"Oh, honestly." Sabrina adjusted a large, undoubtedly very expensive, tooled-leather shoulder bag. "Do you *have* to talk business?"

Alec didn't bother to answer, because anything he said would come out sarcastic. The adrenaline still surged in his veins, and the anger... Best not to dwell on that.

"It is an important part of our trip," Eduardo responded levelly.

Sabrina shrugged. "Where is Fiona, anyway?"

Hiding from you. "In the clubhouse." From the corner of his eye, Alec noticed a black-and-white pulling to the curb.

Good. A police presence ought to put a lid on his ex-wife's mischief.

Or so he'd believed. "Well, let's show her some fun!" She reached for a sparkler. "Eduardo, where's the lighter?"

"Put the fireworks away!" Alec didn't bother to disguise his irritation.

"We went to a lot of trouble to bring these. We had to ship them by rail," Sabrina retorted. "As long as we're here, let's enjoy them."

"Clearly, we have caused a problem. Let us save them for another time." Her companion opened his satchel, allowed Mike to inspect its contents and added the unused poppers and sparklers. "You are very careful about security. I didn't realize Americans were so cautious."

"Only if they're paranoid," Sabrina griped. When Mike indicated her purse, she glared, but opened it at a gesture from Eduardo. "A gift for my daughter. You don't expect me to unwrap it, I hope!"

Mike hesitated, then shook his head. To Alec he said, "I'd better go square things with the police." He strolled off toward the two approaching officers, who greeted him like an old friend.

"Can we go in now?" Sabrina demanded. "You aren't going to have us arrested, are you?"

"Of course not." Alec hung on to his temper. Quarreling would solve nothing.

"I wasn't sure you'd trust us inside without an armed guard." Sabrina stalked forward. In her mile-high heels, she moved like a runway model, clearly aware of the stunning picture she made. The police officers watched her retreating figure as if willing her to turn toward them for a better view.

She's toxic, guys. Don't be an idiot like I was.

Eduardo, however, took more interest in Alec than in his

fiancée as they approached the clubhouse. "I hear Dr. Tartikoff thinks very highly of you. Setting up a laboratory, you must be a technology expert."

"I keep up with the field, yes." Alec still felt reserved around the guy. "You speak excellent English, by the way."

"I earned my MBA at Wharton, in Philadelphia," the man explained. "And I have a second home in New York."

Far away from your wife and children. How could Eduardo bear to be separated from his three kids, who, according to Mike's written report, ranged in age from seven to fifteen? True, the report indicated he visited them occasionally, but he must have been miserable in his marriage to seek a divorce. Or madly in love with Sabrina, in which case he might be putting on a suave front to help her steal her daughter.

Inside the clubhouse, the party was breaking up, Alec saw as they entered. While his mother handed out goody bags, the guests and their stuffed animals were wishing Fiona a happy birthday. Hanging on to Patty, his daughter thanked them all for coming, but her gaze kept straying toward the door.

Toward Sabrina.

Alec registered the mixture of worry and yearning on his daughter's face as her gaze met her mother's. If only he'd chosen more wisely. If only he'd married a woman who valued their child's needs and emotions above her own.

His ex-wife regarded their daughter with a startled expression. "Good heavens, what have they done to your hair? It used to be so beautiful."

Did she have to say that? How insensitive.

Fiona went white, as if she'd been slapped. "I got it cut."

Even Sabrina couldn't be unaware of the frowns directed her way from around the room. Or maybe, Alec thought, she actually registered the fact that she was hurting her daughter. "Once I get used to it, I'm sure I'll love it. Come here, sweetie.

I brought you a present!" Dropping the purse to the floor, she held out her arms.

After a second's hesitation, Fiona trotted forward. Her mother clutched her tightly, and when he moved to get a clear view of Sabrina's face, Alec saw a fiery expression worthy of a tigress.

At some level, his ex-wife did love their daughter, he thought, and it was good for Fiona to experience that. As long as she had him to keep her safe from Sabrina's unpredictable moods.

Patty hovered nearby, closely watching the pair and their surroundings. In this unwavering sentinel, he saw no trace of his goofy high-school sweetheart. She'd become so much more than he'd given her credit for.

Fiona wiggled away from her mother. "Where's my present?"

Out of the purse came a gift box wrapped in elegant pink paper traced with a lace design. Although he hated to disappoint his daughter, Alec knew this wasn't the time. "Fiona, your guests are leaving. You can open it and the rest of your gifts a little later."

His daughter wrinkled her nose at him, but obediently turned her attention to a little girl. "Thanks for coming."

"I had so much fun!"

The two hugged. He hoped some of these new friends would take the place of the ones she'd left behind.

"Oh, honestly!" Sabrina glared at Alec. "You're such a spoilsport. And who's this sourpuss?" She indicated Patty.

A blink was her only reaction to the insult. "I'm the new nanny."

Alec couldn't help noting how different the two women were, despite their similar heights. Sabrina was exotic and high-strung, Patty warm and down-to-earth. Sabrina had all the media-admired photogenic qualities.

Patty had all the soul.

"Where do you find these nannies? You should let me do the hiring," his ex said.

She didn't ask what had happened to the last one. But then, she didn't have to, Alec reflected, if she was the caller who'd scared Tatum away.

Having handed out the last bag of treats, Darlene joined them. "Patty was my choice. I've known her for years. Are you questioning my judgment?"

Sabrina had the sense to keep her mouth shut. She'd ruined many a holiday gathering for his long-suffering parents with her rudeness, temper tantrums and whining. Through it all, Darlene had attempted to keep the peace. But after Sabrina had left Fiona unattended in the car, Darlene had refused to speak to her outside the courtroom except to say, "You are unworthy of my son and undeserving of your daughter."

Apparently Sabrina wasn't eager to hear that opinion repeated in front of Eduardo. Instead, she searched about for another topic of conversation, and fixed on Fiona's stuffed bunny. "You still have Hoppity? Well…that's nice. I've missed *my* little bunny." Turning to her fiancé, she added, "See how cute she is?"

"Precious." Eduardo smiled at the child pleasantly, but with no real interest. "I hope we aren't the reason your guests have fled."

Alec checked his watch. "It's nearly three. That's when the party's supposed to end." He saw appreciatively that Bailey and Tina Torres were bundling the last of the trash into plastic bags. "Guys, we appreciate your help."

"It was fun!" After tying up the bag, the nurse retrieved her purse.

"Thanks for inviting us." Tina and her daughter departed with a wave.

"Good timing," Sabrina said brightly. "Now we're going

to take Fiona to the Page Museum at La Brea Tar Pits, where they have the dinosaurs."

"Saber-toothed tigers and mammoths, not dinosaurs," Darlene interjected.

Her ex-daughter-in-law ignored the correction. "You can't possibly object, Alec. It's educational, and Eduardo can supervise. Dr. Tartikoff *did* phone you about him, didn't he?"

"I assure you, she'll be in excellent hands," the Argentinean added, as Sabrina caught her daughter's arm.

"You aren't taking her anywhere." As Alec moved to block them, anger flashed across Eduardo's face. So much for the show of international goodwill. Perhaps this had been the point of all that friendliness—to put him off his guard. And it came with the veiled threat of making trouble with his boss.

This scene appeared on the verge of turning ugly and, Alec registered with a rush of concern, his little girl was right in the middle of it.

Chapter Sixteen

For Patty, it was a relief to take action. She swooped in, lifted Fiona from her mother's arms and announced, "Anyone can see she's exhausted."

Gratitude shone in Alec's eyes as he moved between Patty and his ex-wife, cutting off her attempt to reclaim their daughter. "Sabrina, why don't you help my mother pack the rest of the presents and refreshments? We'll all feel a lot more comfortable upstairs at my place."

"I do not understand." Eduardo gazed from one to another. "What is the objection to a mother being with her daughter? It is only natural."

"It's a violation of the court's custody order," Alec told him. "After Sabrina left Fiona alone in a car for an hour, the court gave me full custody and limited her to supervised visits. She didn't tell you?"

Obviously not, Patty mused, judging by the frown creasing Eduardo's well-shaped forehead. "Is this so?"

Sabrina shrugged. "It was blown out of proportion. I love my baby! She belongs with me."

"I assure you, I intended no impropriety," Eduardo told Alec. To Sabrina, he said soothingly, "It is better this way, darling. The child is tired, and we have the consul general's party tonight."

That would be in Los Angeles, Alec presumed. Clearly,

this trip had multiple purposes for Eduardo. Presumably he intended to make valuable West Coast trade connections through the Argentine consulate. So his desire to tour the lab might be genuine, after all.

Sabrina started to pout, but seeing her fiancé's raised eyebrow, twisted it into a smile. "All right. We'll visit for a bit today, and tomorrow I'll take my little girl shopping. *If* someone can be bothered to supervise us."

"We'll work it out," Alec said.

Patty was glad to see the tension lifting. Alec was no longer braced as if ready to tackle someone, and Darlene had gone to pack the remaining gifts. After a brief hesitation, Sabrina made a show of going over to help her.

The immediate threat, if that's what it had been, was over. So why did Patty's gut keep insisting she'd overlooked something?

Outside, Mike had sent the patrolmen away. He came in to check on them. "Everything under control?"

"We're fine," Alec said. Patty nodded.

"If it's all right with you, Mr. Denny, I'll swing around the parking lot," Mike continued.

"That will be fine. Thanks."

Patty transferred a drooping Fiona onto Alec's shoulder. "Let me go into the condo first," she murmured, and hurried to catch Mike before he vanished. "Text me an all clear from the parking lot."

"Will do." On the clubhouse steps, he regarded her thoughtfully. "Are you picking up something I missed?"

"Call it instinct." Or was she simply worried because she cared about these people so much?

The stairwell and elevator were clear, and the security camera appeared to be in good condition, Patty noted as the small group followed in her wake. She strode upstairs, letting the others take the elevator. After opening the condo door cautiously, she deactivated the alarm.

A brief tour of the premises showed nothing amiss, and from the balcony she watched Mike inspect the parking lot. Although the row of carports offered spots where someone could hide, she trusted his thoroughness. Plus there were cameras, monitored remotely by the condo's security firm.

Alec brought in Fiona and lowered her to the couch. Sabrina fluttered in with Eduardo, who carried two shopping bags no doubt filled with gifts and refreshments.

"My mother decided not to join us. She's worn-out," Alec told Patty. "How're you doing?"

"Fine." She could feel Sabrina's gaze boring into her, so she said nothing more. Instead, she busied herself putting away a leftover bottle of punch and a plastic container of cupcakes. Apparently all the pizza had been consumed. For once, though, she wasn't interested in eating.

She noted Eduardo watching her. He'd probably figured out she wasn't simply a nanny. What was he up to? She tried to put the pieces together, but they didn't fit any particular pattern. The guy struck her as intelligent and well aware of his position as a wealthy businessman, yet not arrogant. She almost wanted to trust him.

Never underestimate your opponent.

"Anyone care for coffee?" Patty asked, noticing the half-full pot. Although it wasn't her job to serve people, she wanted an excuse to stay in the middle of things.

"I'll pass. But thanks." Alec, who was sticking close to his daughter, shot her an appreciative look.

For today, they'd become a team, coordinating to protect his child. But Patty didn't dare bask in contentment. Instead, she scanned the readout on her phone from Mike: All clear. Still here. It was good that he planned to stick around, because her gut hadn't stopped flashing the warning light.

"No coffee for me." Sabrina took a seat beside Fiona, whose lids were sinking shut. "Honey, aren't you going to open your gift?"

The little girl blinked hard and yawned. "Okay."

"You'll love it!" Sabrina went to the bag and extracted the pink box.

"I would like coffee, please." Eduardo, taking no interest in the proceedings, strolled into the kitchen.

"Coming right up." While Patty heated a mugful in the microwave, he walked to the glass doors that led to the patio, and stood gazing toward the ocean. "Magnificent view."

"It is terrific, isn't it?"

Patty kept her eye on him, although it was hard to picture this gentleman suddenly using karate moves on her. But he could pull a gun.

Behind her, she heard paper ripping. A glance showed Fiona pulling a darling party dress from a nest of multicolored tissue paper and holding it up. It was clearly made for a younger child.

"It's too small," she told her mother.

"You've grown! We've been apart so long, I don't know my own daughter's dress size." Sabrina tapped the shiny box. "I think they have a branch around here. We can exchange it tomorrow, all right?"

Eduardo accepted his coffee, waving away the offer of cream or sugar. "Tomorrow Alec and I will be touring the lab," he pointed out, rejoining his fiancée.

"Darlene can come with us," Sabrina wheedled, turning to Alec. "Honestly, what do you think we're going to do?"

Alec considered, clearly torn. Patty wasn't thrilled about the idea of taking Fiona to such a public place, with or without Sabrina, but she shrugged and left the decision to him.

"All right, if my mother's willing," he said at last. "And Patty will go along, as well."

Sabrina rolled her eyes. "Fine."

"Mommy! Come see my room." Fiona jumped up, energized again, and pulled her mother with her. Patty trailed them, trying to keep alert to what was happening in the living room, should anything go amiss there.

But Eduardo merely talked shop, from what she could hear, inquiring how Alec chose his suppliers, and setting up a time to meet the following day. As for Sabrina, she sat on Fiona's bed and made admiring comments about each toy and picture her daughter showed her. Although it was obvious to Patty that the woman was losing interest, the little girl seemed satisfied.

Finally, Fiona gave a big yawn. "I'm sleepy."

"Why don't you take a nap, dear?" Sabrina helped her remove her shoes and curl under the covers. "I'll see you tomorrow."

"Okay, Mommy. I love you."

"Me, too." Sabrina kissed her on the cheek.

There was no denying the bond between mother and daughter. Patty supposed they would always be connected. Yet there had to be a vital flaw in the woman's character, for her to have endangered Fiona even once.

After a stop in the bathroom, Sabrina emerged with freshened makeup and hair. Scarcely sparing Patty a glance, she went to the living room.

Eduardo's welcoming smile bore admiration for his beautiful fiancée, but he quickly returned his attention to Alec. "In the morning, we will arrive at eleven. You can be ready by then, Sabrina, yes?"

"Sure. Now let's go get ready for the party. What do you think I should wear? The blue sheath or the scarlet silk?" Linking her arm through his, she wiggled her fingers at Alec and sauntered out the door.

"Whatever you wear, my darling, you will look splendid." He spoke with courtesy but, to Patty's ear, not much passion.

When they were gone, Alec locked the door and leaned against it. "Why was that so exhausting? It's not as if anything went wrong."

"Nothing drains you like watching and waiting." Patty would rather lift weights, run a marathon and duke it out with a bad guy than stand around squinting at shadows. "'Scuse me. One more job to do." She took out her phone and called to inform Mike of the couple's departure.

He confirmed his intent to follow them to their hotel, to make sure they didn't double back. "After that, I'm going off duty. Condo security promised to call at any sign of trouble."

"Sounds good. We'll talk tomorrow." Mike deserved his rest, but for Patty, the decision to stay here at night had been the right one. Despite how smoothly things had gone today, she wouldn't sleep tonight if she left.

She wasn't sure she'd sleep, anyway. But there was no reason for Alec to stand around fidgeting or stay awake, rigid with tension. "Sit," Patty commanded, and pointed to a chair.

He gave her a questioning look, but obeyed.

Positioning herself behind him, she began massaging his shoulders. They felt stiff and knotted, as she'd expected. "You're holding on to all that tension. You're not used to being on the alert this way."

"And you are." It was an observation, not a question.

She enjoyed feeling the rumble of his voice through his muscles. "That's how I get my adrenaline fix. Now that it's downtime, you have to learn to breathe deep and let it go." Or take out his frustrations on a punching bag at the gym, but she doubted that was Alec's style.

He rested his head back, his hair tickling her wrists. "Do you think I overreacted?"

"Better safe than sorry." She didn't want to talk about that anymore. She just liked being here with her hands on Alec, working the strain from his body. Probing the strength of his shoulders and the breadth of his back dissolved her own tensions, as well.

"Do you mind?" After a quick sideways smile to gauge her reaction, he moved away and unbuttoned his shirt.

"Fine with me."

More than fine. She loved the feel of his skin beneath her hands. With each stroke along his spine and press of his shoulder blades, she became more connected, more a part of him.

If she was going to stop, she'd better do it now, Patty realized. But she might never again have a chance to get this close. And she wanted it.

Impulsively, she bent down and traced her lips across the roughness of his jaw. He turned, meeting her mouth with his own. When he pulled her onto his lap, she felt herself coming alive as the pressure of his hardness beneath her sent vibrations thrumming through her body. This was what she'd missed with every other man, this joyous sense of anticipation, of belonging in his arms. Returning the probe of his tongue felt perfectly right. She'd waited far too long. They both had.

Patty entertained no illusions about the future. This was foxhole love, the camaraderie of two people under fire. Temporary, and fierce, and precious.

But they weren't alone here. She stopped, her cheek grazing his neck, and forced herself to think like an adult instead of a yearning teenager. "Fiona."

"She's sleeping."

"Taking a nap, that's all." Reluctantly, Patty got to her feet. "She might wake up."

"Hold on." Catching her hand, Alec tugged her into the hall. He peered into his daughter's room, then closed the door quietly. "She'll be out for at least an hour."

"How can you be sure?" Not that Patty didn't hope he was right.

"I recognize the signs. And one thing I've learned about being a parent is that you can't put your life on hold for the next twenty years." He cupped her cheek in his palm. "We both need this."

"No promises," she warned. "No expectations."

"You're the weirdest woman I ever met. You should be requiring my signature on a declaration of intent," Alec teased, guiding her toward his bedroom.

She should be doing a lot of things, Patty mused through a haze of desire. Barricading herself in her room. Taking a cold shower. Reminding herself that Alec was her client.

Life was too short to worry about all that. "Oh, hell, let's go for it," she said.

In the bedroom, after locking the door, they drew back the quilt. "We get a whole bed," Patty marveled. "Remember going at it in your car?"

"How could I forget? I have a permanent kink in my back." He grinned as he lifted her top over her head. "Hmm, I kind of like having your arms pinned this way." Unhooking her bra, he brought his mouth to her breasts, sending heat into places Patty had nearly forgotten she possessed.

When he lifted his head, she squirmed out of the top, wriggled out of the bra and pulled him onto the bed. He began kissing her all over. Oh, man, the sensation was beyond divine.

What was it that nagged at her brain? Oh, yeah. "Wallet," she murmured.

"Excuse me?" Alec regarded her questioningly.

"Protection." She might not need it very often, but Patty always carried one with her. Badge, gun, condom. She'd said goodbye to the first two, but not the latter.

"Right." He helped her locate her slacks and the condom. She'd never imagined she could enjoy the process of stretching it over a man's erection, but with Alec...well, with Alec, everything was different.

Everything.

The sense of being truly part of him. The discovery that she enjoyed his reactions, his moans, his speeding heartbeat as much as her own. The wonder that she was actually here with Alec inside her, and the amazement that she'd survived without him for so long.

Then they fused completely. Lightning flashed and the world shimmered. Patty held on to the glorious moment as long as she could, and held on to Alec even after the storm abated, leaving a rainbow arcing across a clear blue sky.

Curled around her, he said, "I never..." The words trailed off.

That about summed it up. "Yeah, me, either."

"We're like cells that hook into one another." Alec tightened his grip on her. "It's as if we have receptors especially encoded for each other."

"No biology talk," Patty told him.

He laughed. "I can't help it."

"We did enough biology for one evening." Not exactly true. "Well, for an hour, anyway." But they wouldn't have time for another round. Recalled to duty, she sat up. "We'd better get dressed before our little pal comes calling."

Alec stopped her with a hand on her arm. "Forgive me?"

"Hey, you weren't that bad," she joked.

He gave her a light poke. "I mean for my stupidity in high school. I made a terrible mistake."

Much as she wanted to accept that it was true, Patty forced herself to be practical. "You aren't thinking straight. Maybe we could have made it together, maybe not, but what we did tonight, well, that was just releasing some pressure."

In the faint, late-afternoon light, his eyes grew dark and unreadable. "Is that all this meant to you?"

What did he expect, a declaration of undying love? "It was great. The best. But as far as anything further, let's keep it real."

Her chest gave a painful squeeze. *Liar.*

But Patty couldn't be anyone except who she was, the ex-cop, the no-holds-barred lady on a skateboard who didn't fit the life Alec had chosen. The director of laboratories. The handsome man in a suit. Sooner or later, he would remember why he'd broken up with her in the first place.

He made no move toward his clothes. "I imagined we meant more than that to each other."

She turned away to hide the hurt. Yes, he meant more to her than a one-night stand. Too much more. Too much to risk that looming moment when, sooner or later, he realized that his intense emotions were only a reaction to the sense of danger and the enforced intimacy. That he might like being alone with her, but he didn't want his colleagues to associate him with this rough-edged woman.

"You'll always be special to me, Alec." Her voice sounded gruff in her ears.

"But you're only here because my daughter's in danger," he finished for her.

"Close enough."

The creak of a floorboard in the hall sent her bolt upright, even before a tiny voice called, "Daddy?"

"Hold on a sec, sweetheart." Alec fumbled for his clothes, while Patty dressed in record time, even for her.

She left it to Alec to make an excuse. He opened the door and said, "We all had a nice nap. You hungry?"

"Yeah!"

After omelets and a salad, Fiona asked for the rest of her gifts. She settled happily in the living room, tearing the wrappings off the packages. Darlene had selected doctor and nurse dolls and a couple of DVDs. Patty was glad to see Fiona grin on receiving the book she'd picked out for her, *A Day at the Police Station*. But the obvious favorite came from Alec, a junior microscope set with a kit and book so Fiona could make her own slides.

"Can I use it now?" the little girl begged.

Alec glanced at Patty. "Go ahead. I'll clean up in here," she told him.

"Wait." He scraped a tiny sample of the leftovers onto a plate. "We can start by looking at this up close and personal."

With a whoop of joy, Fiona helped him carry her new gear into her room. A young scientist in the making.

So the birthday had a happy ending, after all, Patty mused as she cleared the plates and went into the living room to remove the torn paper and ribbons. As she lifted the shopping bag that had held the gifts, she was surprised to feel enough weight to indicate they'd overlooked one.

From inside, she took out a flat package wrapped in elegant pink paper covered with a lacy pattern. Another present from Sabrina, or perhaps Eduardo. Curious, Patty debated for a moment, then slid off the shiny ribbon and loosened the tape on the back so the wrappings could be refastened without much damage.

From inside, Patty drew a book. Her breath caught as she read the title.

The Kid's Guide to Living Abroad.

Opening it with a sense of apprehension, she read the single word written on the flyleaf: *Soon!*

Chapter Seventeen

On Sunday morning, Alec awoke and reached out with sleepy contentment. For a moment, as his hand met empty space in the bed, he wondered when Patty had arisen, and then he remembered.

She'd turned down his effort to bridge the gap between them, and spent the night in her own room. The scent that infused his senses was left from yesterday afternoon's lovemaking.

Was she right about this powerful desire being a reaction to the intensity of their situation? He couldn't be certain. For today, he had no choice but to accept Patty's decision. Besides, he had more urgent matters to deal with.

Just when he'd figured his ex-wife's threats were nothing more than bluster, that book with the ominous inscription had turned up. More drama—typical of Sabrina. After he and Patty discussed it last night, they'd agreed not to make an issue of it today, but to remain on red alert.

Prying himself from the cozy bed, Alec peeked out. The smell of coffee told him Patty had beaten him to the punch, and he heard his daughter's voice chirping from the front room. She seemed to be introducing her new dolls and bear to Hoppity and the old gang. All safe, for now.

He checked the clock. Nearly ten. How had he slept so late?

Alec hurried to shower. Much as he hated to be separated

from his daughter today, he'd promised to show Eduardo around the lab. After postponing the visit because of the birthday party, he could hardly explain to Owen that he'd alienated a potential research sponsor because he felt an urge to play security guard.

Patty was on duty. So was Mike, who'd agreed to follow Fiona at a discreet distance when she went out in public, even though, as it turned out, she and Patty wouldn't be mall hopping with Sabrina. When Alec had called Darlene after dinner to make sure she'd recovered from her exhaustion, she'd felt fine, but informed him that she, Patty and Fiona had a lunch date, and she didn't intend to let Sabrina interfere. "Shopping? She'd bore that child and the rest of us to death trying on clothes for herself. We can meet her at your place after lunch."

He'd reached his ex on her cell. Caught up in the excitement of the party, she'd agreed to the change with a minimum of grumbling. Now that she knew their daughter's latest size, she'd said, she could shop by herself and bring everything over later. She hadn't even asked how Fiona had liked the book. That was typical of Sabrina, to stir up trouble and then put it out of her mind.

After his shower, Alec shaved and then stood in front of his closet, debating whether to wear a suit. It seemed ridiculous on a Sunday, so he settled for slacks and a sport coat. In Southern California, that was practically formal wear, anyway.

He wondered briefly if Eduardo meant to spring some surprise on him—tie him up at the lab, perhaps? But like yesterday's fireworks commotion, the book inscription probably amounted to nothing.

Opening the door to the hallway, he heard Fiona say, "Can we have pancakes?"

The voice that answered was Darlene's. "For lunch? I don't think so."

"But I had a sandwich for breakfast!"

Cooking was not Patty's forte, Alec reflected with amusement as he emerged to see the three of them sitting around the table, playing cards. A sandwich for breakfast? His guess: peanut butter.

"Hello, son," Darlene said cheerfully. "Fiona's teaching us the game Rosita showed her. That woman's amazing. She stopped by this morning on her way to church to make sure I was feeling well and to find out how the party went."

"Hi, Daddy!" Without waiting for her grandmother to finish speaking, Fiona leaped up, scattering her cards, and hurled herself across the room. When he swept her into a hug, his little angel bestowed butterfly kisses on his cheeks. Tears of love pricked Alec's eyes.

Patty good-naturedly scraped the deck together. "She couldn't remember all the rules, anyway."

"But we were having fun," Darlene teased.

"Yeah, I like games where you make up the rules as you go," Patty agreed.

"Where are you planning to eat lunch?" Releasing his daughter, Alec went to pour himself a cup of coffee.

"Patty's choice," his mother said.

Fiona scooted over to her. "Pancakes! Pancakes!"

"I was thinking maybe health food," Patty said, deadpan.

Big brown eyes gazed up at her. "No sprouts! Please."

"Or foreign cuisine." Patty cocked her head as if deep in thought. "French? Dutch? I know! Belgian."

Darlene regarded her askance. Fiona looked uncertain, too.

Then Alec got it. "As in, Belgian waffles?"

"There has to be calcium in that whipped cream they put on the top, with the nuts and syrup," Patty said.

Fiona gave a jump. "Yay!"

Darlene chuckled. "I guess I'm outvoted."

"I'm sure they serve whole-grain picklewurst if you really want some," Patty told her solemnly.

His mother burst out laughing. "I hope you made that up because it sounds awful."

"Yeah." Patty grinned. "We gals are gonna have a good time."

He didn't doubt it, Alec reflected as he took a yogurt from the fridge. "Wish I could join you. Still, I'm curious to see Eduardo's reaction to the lab."

"Seems odd to me," said Patty. "I mean, that a businessman from Argentina would consider investing in American medical research."

"Networking with potential markets for their technology could be very valuable to the Patron family. And our program will be glad to get sponsors, wherever we can find them." Alec leaned against the counter.

"Sponsors for what, exactly?" Darlene asked.

"Owen Tartikoff's always looking for a fresh approach, some way to rev up the fertility rate, and if it involves a new medical device or technique, all the better. Something as simple as increasing the percentage of nitrogen versus oxygen in the air while culturing embryos has made a significant improvement in the outcome. So to answer your question, yes, Eduardo's interest might be genuine."

Or it might not. He still wished, fervently, that he could stick close to them today. "What time does Mike come on duty?" It was nearly eleven now, he realized.

"Five minutes ago. He texted me that he's outside," Patty said.

"By the time we're seated and served, it'll be nearly noon." Darlene shot Fiona a meaningful glance. "Better put on your shoes and wash your hands."

"Yes, Grandma!" The little girl pelted off.

"Have fun." Alec took a deep breath, and his gaze met Patty's in shared understanding. For today, they were united in purpose.

As for any chance of them staying together after this was over, that would have to wait.

PATTY KEPT A SHARP WATCH as she shepherded Darlene and a chatty Fiona out of the condo. The sight of Mike sitting in his car at the curb should have reassured her, but she couldn't shake the nagging sense of something working beneath the surface.

If Sabrina had hired an accomplice, he or she had no doubt figured out the basic security arrangements and made efforts to counter them. She wished Mike's brother Lock had arrived, so they could throw in a new person less readily identifiable, but he was still laid up in Flagstaff while his leg mended.

A child could be easily whisked away from Southern California. Driven to the Mexican border less than two hours to the south, hustled into an airplane and flown out of the country, or bundled onto a boat. Pleasure craft from the local harbor weren't monitored, nor were flight plans.

In other words, if people with access to Eduardo's wealth got their hands on Fiona, they had a good chance of smuggling her out of the United States. So, as a precaution, Patty drove a circuitous route to Waffle Heaven, located in the same commercial strip as the Suncrest Supermarket. Once inside, she slipped the hostess a large tip and explained quietly that they were in a hurry. She also requested a booth in a back corner from which she could scan the entire room.

They were seated almost immediately. While Patty felt a twinge of guilt at moving ahead of several large groups of brunch goers, it was important to spend as little time here as possible.

She'd almost forgotten the reason for this get-together until, after they placed their orders, Darlene said, "I'm glad we have this chance to chat, the three of us."

"Four." Fiona held up her new teddy, Blue Boy, named for the color of the ribbon around his neck.

"I hope he knows how to behave in public," Patty remarked. "You never can tell with a new bear. Some of them have no manners at all."

Fiona giggled.

"Exactly," Darlene said.

"Exactly what?" Patty asked.

"Exactly why you're wonderful with my granddaughter," she stated.

"Thanks." Patty noted a single man being escorted to a nearby table. That was odd—you didn't usually see a guy dining solo at Sunday brunch. Nor did the gray hair rule him out as a potential threat.

Briefly returning her attention to Darlene, she said, "You aren't under the impression that I'm available for full-time nanny duty, are you?"

The grandmother's laugh rolled through the restaurant. "That isn't even close to what I meant."

"Sorry. What *did* you mean?" Ah, here came a jaunty woman to join the single guy. Not suspicious, after all.

"I wanted you to know that I approve of whatever you and my son decide to do." Darlene folded her hands on the table.

Patty had no idea what that meant. "You mean, if we hire a gorilla as her next nanny, that would be okay?"

"A gorilla?" Fiona's eyes widened. "Oh. You're *kidding*."

"I don't think our little girl needs another nanny," Darlene went on calmly. "She's ready for preschool. Besides, I was thinking more in terms of a step…"

A waitress materialized, balancing three large platters. "Who had the Walnut Maple Surprise?"

Was Darlene Denny, who'd once scowled at the mere sight of Patty, suggesting that she would welcome her as a daughter-in-law? Patty was so astounded that she couldn't remember what she'd ordered. Fortunately, the others were able to identify their platters.

"The Pineapple Express must be yours." The waitress slid the plate onto the table in front of Patty.

"Yes," she said. It must be, since it was the only one left.

After the waitress left, Darlene sat toying with her fork. "A girl needs to grow up with a role model."

"Me?" Patty had never envisioned herself in that light. "I don't own a pair of panty hose and if there are multiple forks beside my plate, I pick one at random."

"I'm talking about a woman who shows integrity. Loyalty. Responsibility," Darlene said. "That's the kind of woman Alec should have married. I hope you don't mind my speaking so plainly."

"Not at all." How ironic that Darlene had given her blessing, twelve years late. Patty hoped the woman wasn't going to be too disappointed when she and Alec went their separate ways.

Clearing her throat, she surveyed the restaurant again. Still no obvious danger. She dug into her waffles, eating fast out of habit. On duty, you never knew when you might be interrupted.

Fiona couldn't finish, and begged to take her leftovers in a carton. "It's for Hoppity. He misses me."

"I wondered how long Blue Boy would stay in favor," Patty said. "I mean, new is fun, but old friends are the best."

"They certainly are," Darlene replied, and signaled the waitress.

Eight minutes past twelve. They'd finished eating early, which was fine with Patty. The sooner they got safely home, the better.

"DR. GIOVANNI'S LAB in Buenos Aires is not nearly so extensive." Eduardo, who'd alternated between admiring exclamations and pointed questions, paused at a newly installed workspace. "This clear hood, it reminds me of what you see in a salad bar. To keep customers from breathing on the food."

"It serves the same function here," Alec agreed. Around them, the hospital basement lay silent and empty on a Sunday. "It's called a laminar flow hood. There's a built-in fan to keep the air circulating in a pattern that reduces contamination while we handle reproductive material."

The Argentinean, who'd worn a magenta silk shirt and gray tailored slacks, spread his hands expressively. "I wish my family had not insisted I pursue business. I love science." He'd already explained how overjoyed he was about the purchase of a small biotech firm, and how he wished to educate himself in the field.

"This is the lab that's closest to completion. There's not much to look at in the others unless you're fascinated by pipes and drywall. Do you want to tour the rest of the hospital?" Alec had explained earlier how they were fitting their program into the existing structure.

"Not today, thank you." The visitor seemed in no hurry to leave, however. "My older son, Eduardo, is only fifteen, but very advanced in his studies. He talks of going to university in the U.S. I have heard good reports of the biology program at UC Irvine, but after this visit, I think he should look elsewhere."

"What changed your mind? It's a very attractive campus."

"Oh, yes, and excellent faculty. But this area has a high crime rate, no?"

"Orange County?" Alec wondered where on earth the man got his information. "We have our share of crimes, but the overall rate is fairly low."

"Yet you must hire such security for your daughter's birth-day party." Eduardo showed no hint of irony.

Was the man trying to provoke a response, or was he truly unaware of the situation? Alec decided to level with him. "I hired a guard because, about a week ago, Sabrina threatened to take our daughter to Argentina."

"But I thought the court does not allow this," the man responded, with what appeared to Alec to be genuine dismay.

"It doesn't."

He could see understanding dawn. "All this—the guard, and this formidable nanny—this is because of Sabrina? But surely you know she makes wild statements when she is upset."

Either this fellow was an incredibly smooth operator or he was being frank. Alec decided to be equally forthcoming. "She didn't say these things just to me. Our previous nanny quit last week after Sabrina called and threatened her."

"I cannot believe this." The man held up a hand as if to forestall an argument. "I do not question your honesty. And I would react strongly also if my wife made a threat about our children."

Alec decided to steer the conversation to safer ground. "You mentioned your older son, but you have two younger ones, don't you?"

"Franco is ten. My youngest, Mona, is only seven. Your daughter reminds me of her."

And yet you choose to live on the other side of the world. "Don't you miss them?"

"I went to school in the U.S. My family—extended family, as you would say—expects me to represent them here." He sounded wistful.

"Surely you'll see them even less when you're divorced."

The other man's gaze fixed on a framed photograph on the wall, one of a series showing babies sitting and crawling, wearing floppy hats and cute costumes. "I have fire in my blood, and I follow my passions. This, I have always believed, is the path to happiness, but lately I am not so sure."

"You're having second thoughts about the divorce?" Alec knew he was prying, but the other man didn't seem to mind.

Eduardo shrugged. "This weekend, seeing your daughter, it makes me think of my children. And my wife. She is a remarkable woman. Very beautiful in her day."

"We have a saying," Alec told him. "Beauty fades. Character lasts."

"Perhaps you are right. But beauty is to be treasured also." At the sound of a beep, Eduardo took his phone from his pocket. "It is a text from Sabrina."

Alec's indifference turned to concern as he watched the other man stare at the screen. "How can this be?" Eduardo shook his head as if dazed.

"What?" His throat tightening with alarm, Alec reached out. The other man handed him the phone without argument.

Sabrina's message was short and appalling.

I choose my daughter over you. Goodbye.

Chapter Eighteen

Despite Mike's car following half a block behind, Patty drove home edgily aware of the other vehicles around them, ready to take evasive action if there were any sudden moves. Beside her, Darlene drummed her fingers on her knee.

"I'm sorry," she finally said.

"For what?" Patty kept her gaze trained on the road.

"You haven't spoken a word since we left the restaurant. I offended you, didn't I?"

"Not at all," Patty said. "Just doing my job."

"You really think someone might…?" Darlene didn't finish the sentence.

"That's why I'm here."

In the rear seat, Fiona leaned forward as if trying to make the car go faster. "Hoppity is hungry," she said. "He's waiting for the leftovers."

The child must have felt the stress, too, and needed the comfort of her favorite toy. With luck, they'd be home in a minute.

Not seeing anyone around, Patty drove into the condo's visitor lot. Sabrina wasn't expected for nearly another two hours, so they had plenty of leeway.

Mike parked on the street. He would keep watch and make the occasional patrol around the grounds again today. Eduardo and Sabrina had said they planned to return to New York on

Monday morning, but Patty took nothing for granted. She'd stay on duty as long as Alec needed her.

After that, there were cases to handle, friends to see, a busy life to lead. And she'd need it, because as soon as their foxhole intimacy ended, Alec was going to return to his own busy schedule.

Well, let the future take care of itself. She had to stay focused on the present.

Patty didn't see anyone lurking near the stairs, which was a good thing, because Fiona shot ahead of her and raced up the steps. "Wait!" Patty pelted after her, leaving Darlene to take the elevator.

The little girl was so eager to reach her beloved bunny that she took off running across the portico before Patty could grab her. Lacking a key, Fiona was going to have to wait by the door, but Patty mistrusted an uncontrolled situation. Especially with a child involved.

Ahead, Fiona reached for the door handle. To Patty's shock, it turned, and the little girl disappeared inside.

"Fiona!" She leaped forward, her mind skittered over possibilities. Alec might have returned early, but why would he?

Before darting inside, Patty turned to signal Mike, but she couldn't see him from here, and didn't want to pause to use the phone. Then, at the other end of the portico, Darlene emerged from the elevator. "Call 9-1-1! The door's unlocked!" Patty cried. The startled woman nodded and reached into her purse.

Patty entered with caution and ducked to one side. No bullets flew, but from the bedroom hallway burst a tall, thin, dark-haired figure pulling a shrieking Fiona behind her.

After a quick, fierce glance at Patty through tangled hair, Sabrina cut across the condo toward the balcony.

"Stop!" Wearing running shoes instead of high heels gave Patty a speed advantage, but she couldn't move fast in the confined space. The other woman yanked open the balcony door and dodged out, her daughter in her wake. And Hoppity. Somehow the stuffed animal seemed to be wedged between them.

If Patty didn't stop them, Sabrina would escape over the edge of the balcony and onto the carport roof. And there might be an accomplice or at least a car waiting below.

Didn't she care that Fiona might be injured?

Obviously, her daughter's safety wasn't the woman's priority.

For all her planning, Patty hadn't foreseen that Sabrina would find a way past their locks and alarms and lie in wait. She was obviously more desperate, and crazier, than anyone had imagined.

POWERED BY ADRENALINE, Alec pushed the speed limit through the streets of Safe Harbor, with Eduardo tensely silent at his side. He hadn't been able to get through on Patty's phone to warn her, and his mother's was busy. He didn't even know for sure where Fiona was right now, but his instincts told him to head for the condo.

Then he remembered Mike. Chafing with impatience at a red light, Alec pressed the man's number in his cell.

The detective answered promptly, "Mr. Denny? I think something's wrong. Your mother's waving at me from the second-floor walkway. I'm going up now. Call the police."

Alec dialed 9-1-1 and, after watching for cross traffic, hit the gas. Never mind whether he got a ticket.

"Yes, sir, we just received a call from that location," the dispatcher said when he reached her. "Reporting a possible break-in. We're rolling on it now." She sounded much too calm for his taste.

"Someone's kidnapping my five-year-old daughter!" He

didn't mention his ex-wife. If the police assumed this was a custody matter, they might not treat it as urgent.

"I'll alert the units. Hold the line, please."

She returned a moment later and asked a few more questions. By the time Alec finished identifying himself and providing other background, he'd reached his street.

As he clicked off, he saw Eduardo staring at the text message still visible on his own screen. "Now, this is odd."

"What is?" Alec peered anxiously ahead as he drove the last block.

"The message, it's from Sabrina's old phone."

Alec hit the brakes and turned sharply into the condo driveway. "I thought that got stolen."

"So did I." Eduardo tapped a few keys. "Let me try her new phone."

Alec failed to see the point, but didn't object. On the upstairs portico, he spotted his mother pacing outside his condo's open doorway. No sign of Mike. Where was Fiona? Where was Patty?

In the distance, he heard a siren, but he didn't plan to sit here and wait for reinforcements. Since presumably Mike had gone inside, Alec opened the gate so he could drive around back. If Sabrina had broken into his place and tried to escape via the balcony, he'd cut her off.

"Hello?" Eduardo said into the phone. "Yes, where are you?"

Alec rounded a corner and nearly choked at the sight of Patty leaning dangerously over the railing above them, struggling with Sabrina. Fiona was boxed into a corner, holding tight to her stuffed rabbit. A man loomed in the opening and made a grab for the child, but she shrank away.

From the corner of his eye, he caught a movement from Eduardo. Alec flinched, but the man was only holding up his phone. "It's Sabrina. She says she's in a dressing room at Nordstrom."

Alec stared up at the dark-haired woman, her spine pressed against the railing as she clawed at Patty. "Then who…" His voice catching in his throat, he had to force the words out. "Who the hell is that?"

"*CHICA ESTÚPIDA! IDIOTA!* Get off me, you stupid girl!"

Ignoring a stream of insults in Spanish and English, Patty fended off a fingernail attack despite the blood streaming down her arms from earlier scratches.

Behind her, Mike finally managed to pull a terrified Fiona inside. Common sense told Patty to ease off, now that the child was safe, but five years on the police force had conditioned her to bring in her man, or woman. Especially a nasty piece of work like Rosita.

"Come in quietly and explain…" The woman was hoisting herself onto the railing, ready to jump. "Don't you dare!" With a lunge, Patty caught the culprit around the hips.

Who'd figure a bone-thin creature like this would possess such strength? Struggling for balance, Patty refused to release her, fueled by the image of Fiona being hauled onto the balcony. If Patty failed to drag this perpetrator to justice, they'd never be able to prove that Sabrina had hired her. It didn't exactly make sense, to plop a dark wig—now seriously crooked—on Rosita, but since when had Alec's ex been known for clear thinking?

As if in slow motion, Patty registered the tipping point. One instant she was firmly braced, and the next their balance shifted and it dawned on her that they were both going over the rail.

What was Spanish for "say your prayers"? Patty wondered, and prepared to tumble and roll.

ALEC'S PROFOUND RELIEF at seeing his daughter safe vanished at the realization that Patty faced a serious fall. He bolted from the car, trying to calculate where she'd land. Thank goodness she'd separated herself from the other woman's flailing descent.

Everything else faded—the approaching sirens, the kidnapper's screams—as he watched Patty impact the sloped carport roof. She rolled at an angle, somersaulted and went feetfirst over the edge. Knees bent, Alec reached out, fearing for a moment that he'd misjudged the distance, and then connected, absorbing some of the shock as they both collapsed onto the concrete.

As he gingerly sat up, he could feel a vivid array of bruises forming, but nothing seemed broken. "Patty? Patty?" She lay heavily against him, stunned but breathing.

Her eyes blinked and slowly focused on him. "Hey, Alec. Nice catch."

He hugged her close, torn between an urge to sob with relief and an equally powerful urge to laugh. Trust Patty to take a life-threatening fall with aplomb.

The other woman hadn't been so lucky. While the carport had helped break her drop, she'd landed hard. She lay crumpled beside a dark wig that had fallen away to reveal streaky gray hair.

"Good Lord," Alec said as recognition dawned. "It's Rosita."

"Who?" Eduardo knelt beside the intruder, his face a study in distress. "How can this be? Paloma!"

Alec recalled hearing that name before. "Your wife?"

"*Sí.*" Bending over her, Eduardo asked plaintively, "*Porqué?* Why have you done this?"

"*Para ti, mi amor. Te amo,*" she whispered, and went limp.

THIS WAS EDUARDO'S long-suffering wife? Patty almost sympathized, especially since she thought for a moment the woman had died. But those long lashes fluttered open again, then hovered picturesquely at half-mast. Talk about your drama queen!

Used to be a soap opera actress, Mike had said. *Why didn't I pick up on that?* Patty figured Rosita had lied about being related to Marla, so why hadn't it occurred to her she might have lied about other things, too?

"You sure you're all right?" Alec was asking, his arms tight around her. "You took quite a beating."

Patty's legs ached and her arms smarted from the deep scratches. "No big deal. How's Fiona?"

"Mike's got her." Sure enough, she saw her boss peering down from the second floor. When a small face appeared beside him, Mike shook his head apologetically, then escorted her inside.

Much as she enjoying lying here nestled against Alec, Patty didn't deserve his tenderness. She'd let him down. Not only had she not been suspicious of Rosita, she'd allowed the child to dash into the condo first. Sure, things had worked out in the end, but the image of Fiona being dragged onto the balcony remained seared into her brain.

Rosita—make that Paloma—lay on the pavement, clearly in pain but talking rapidly in Spanish to her husband. With a slight stagger, Patty got up, using Alec's shoulder for support. "Hope I didn't mash you too bad when I fell," she told him.

He rose stiffly. "Nothing a hot bath won't fix. When I saw you up there…honey, I thought— If anything had happened to you…"

…it would be no more than I deserve. Patty swallowed the words, because Eduardo was addressing them. "She says she wanted to make Sabrina look bad, so I would return to my family. I apologize. It is my fault for driving my wife over the brink. She was mad with love for me."

"And that justifies her invading my home and attacking my daughter?" Alec demanded.

"It is an accident," Paloma protested. "I make sure the security cameras see me, see Sabrina. Then I pin a note to the rabbit, a promise to come for my daughter. When I hear someone enter, I run. I think my hand must freeze on the toy. Fiona grabs it and somehow…" She ended with a shrug.

Patty supposed that made sense. So did a lot of things, now that she understood Mrs. Patron's plan. As housekeeper, Paloma had had a key and the security codes, as well as an opportunity to plant the children's book. As for the cell-phone threat and the identical wrapping paper… "You broke into their apartment in New York?"

"I do not have to break in," Paloma insisted. "It belongs to me, also."

"But Rosita Martin really exists. Mike checked her ID."

The woman's face contorted in pain, and she clutched her leg. What had she expected trying to escape over a second-floor balcony? After a moment, though, she managed to say, "Rosita Martin writes me many fan letters. I tell her I need to pose as housekeeper to research new role."

"You tricked a fan into helping you pull this scam?" Alec asked.

"Not a scam! I do this for love." Paloma broke off as two police officers hurried around the corner. At the sight of their uniforms, she put up her hands. "I surrender."

"We need paramedics," Patty announced.

As they called for aid, two more officers showed up, Bill Sanchez and George Green. "Look who's here!" George called. "Hiya, Pats."

"You are not really a nanny," Paloma observed.

Oh, great. Did she have to mention that in front of this pair?

"A nanny?" Bill snorted. "Patty used to be a great cop and

now she's a detective. Pretty good pool player, too. So when's the big match with Leo, anyway?"

"Soon." Patty couldn't think about that now.

"Okay," Bill said. "What exactly is going on here, anyway?"

That, she mused, was going to be a long story.

THE PARAMEDICS PATCHED UP Patty's scratches, but since she was current on her tetanus shot, she declined further treatment. Paloma Patron, who appeared to have broken a leg, along with suffering numerous bruises, was sent to the hospital under guard. She faced charges of burglary, assault, child endangerment and whatever else the district attorney could throw at her.

Fiona seemed shaken but pleased when Patty assured her that she'd been remarkably brave in rescuing Hoppity. The little girl, seated securely in her father's lap, confirmed that she'd deliberately hung on to the stuffed animal.

"Why did Rosita try to steal my bunny?" she asked after the officers, who'd taken statements and searched the rooms, went to check Darlene's condo for any evidence Paloma might have left.

"Because he's so cute," Patty said. "Don't worry. It won't happen again."

"Because you're here?" the little girl asked.

"Your dad's here. And your grandma." Darlene had gone downstairs with the police. "I'm afraid I have to pack and go home, because I'm not really a nanny."

"There's no hurry," Alec said.

"I'm on the clock," she reminded him.

"My ex-wife's still in town, you'll recall."

Amazing how that had slipped her mind. Patty couldn't indulge her impulse to retreat, not yet. "Of course. I'll stay as long as you like. In the meantime, you should change your security code right away. Your mother should do the same. And get a locksmith out here ASAP to rekey your locks."

"Good idea. I wonder if they work on Sundays." Alec was looking up a locksmith's number when Sabrina arrived with a shopping bag full of children's clothes to replace the too-small gift. Fiona greeted her eagerly, but as soon as Sabrina learned what had happened and that Eduardo had rushed to the hospital to see his estranged wife, she roared off after only the briefest of farewells.

With tears in her eyes, Fiona stood clutching the bag. "She doesn't want to see how they look on me?"

As Alec gave his daughter a hug, Patty's heart ached for the little girl. Sabrina was still Fiona's mother in spite of everything, and always would be, however flawed. *And perhaps no more flawed than I am.*

Patty's uneasiness grew, not because she sensed any further danger but because she'd come so closing to failing everyone. Fiona. Alec. Even Mike. But she had a job to do here and now, and it was no use wallowing in recriminations.

The afternoon proved hectic, with a locksmith coming in at double his usual rate, the police dropping by with further questions, and Eduardo stopping off to apologize for all the trouble. According to him, Paloma had confessed to hiring a detective to learn as much as possible about her rival. When she'd learned of the situation with Fiona, she'd drawn on a previous role as a housemaid in a TV show to take on the part in real life.

"I don't know how she pulled it off. Obviously, she's wild with passion for me," he said with a mixture of admiration and wonder. "How can I resist such a woman? And now it appears she may go to prison. I must stand by her through this ordeal."

"You're reconciling?" Alec asked. "How'd that go over with Sabrina?"

"Not well," the man admitted. "She is flying back to New York this evening. I have asked her to move her things from my apartment. I believe she plans to stay with her parents."

"That ought to be fun," Alec muttered.

"Such a beautiful woman. I am sure she will find a new man soon."

Patty didn't doubt it.

Finally things quieted down. After dinner, Mike confirmed Sabrina's departure on board a flight to New York. And Alec, with some reluctance, released Patty from her work assignment.

Fiona seemed exhausted. Once they'd tucked her into bed and finished reading her the police station book, Patty packed her belongings.

As she emerged into the living room, Alec looked up from the couch. He closed his laptop and set it aside. "I realize there's no reason for you to stay here, but this isn't the end for you and me. I hope it's just the beginning."

Her heart should have leaped at those words, but Patty couldn't accept them. Neither did she want to dwell on her regret at what a poor showing she'd made. Alec, being kind-hearted, would probably dismiss it and thank her again, as he'd already done several times. Even Mike had overlooked her mistakes, embarrassed by his own failure to probe deeper into Rosita's identity.

Nobody blamed Patty for how close Fiona had come to disaster. Nobody but Patty herself. She had to work even harder, perfect her skills and double her alertness, to prove she deserved other people's trust.

"I can't do this," she told Alec, keeping the width of the room between them. "It's been fun. You're a great guy. I'm glad we finally, well, got together. But we can't go back to where we were because we aren't the same people."

"I don't expect that…."

"I've gotta go. Long day ahead of me at work tomorrow." She forced a smile, made an attempt at a casual wave, and turned her back on Alec's hurt, dismayed, yearning expression.

Chapter Nineteen

That week took on a surreal quality for Alec. A website in Argentina found out about Paloma's risk-everything-for-love venture from the real Rosita Martin, and played it up as the tragic romantic tale of a wronged wife.

Still, with a badly broken leg and other injuries, Paloma hadn't escaped unscathed. So Alec didn't object when he heard the district attorney's office was considering a plea bargain that might result in a suspended sentence and deportation.

Eduardo remained interested in future research projects, much to Dr. Tartikoff's satisfaction. Alec was willing to work with the man as long as he kept his wife out of the country.

Since he had no desire to hire another nanny, Alec began taking his daughter to the hospital's day-care center. He enrolled her in the summer session of a highly recommended local preschool, which would begin in a few weeks.

At home, Fiona moped around the condo, playing only sporadically with her new toys and taking little interest in her pretty clothes. She kept asking when they were going to see Patty again, and Alec had to admit he didn't know. To her credit, Patty sent the girl funny cartoon emails every day through Darlene, but that was no substitute for having her around. Sabrina's departure didn't seem to affect the child nearly as much as Patty's.

Alec could have sworn his mother was moping, too. She'd

fired Marla, who conceded Paloma had paid for a recommendation, but said she'd believed her claim to be the highly qualified Rosita. Darlene arranged instead to hire a housekeeper from a licensed, bonded agency. She also announced that she'd discovered the name of the card game *casita robada* meant "robbed house."

"Appropriate, isn't it? Tell Patty. She'll get a good laugh out of it," Darlene said. "She has such healthy attitudes about things. She's refreshing."

Alec didn't mention their last conversation. Learning that Patty had rejected the idea of a continuing relationship could only hurt his mother and daughter. And he kept hoping that, with time, she might reconsider.

Through Fact Hunter Investigations, Patty submitted a dry, factual report, while Mike handled all verbal communications. Alec's personal calls to Patty's cell phone went unreturned.

When they'd made love, he could have sworn she'd felt the same intense connection he did. So what was holding her back?

No matter how much he missed her, though, he had to respect her feelings and her distance.

For now.

ON TUESDAY, Patty photographed a cheating husband entering and exiting a motel room with his secretary. On Wednesday, she was able to notify the parents of the runaway teenage boy that he'd been hiding out at an older guy's house, where the pair appeared to be addicted to video games. He'd missed the final few weeks of school, and would no doubt spend his summer making up for it.

With the extra money she'd earned over the weekend, she was tempted to buy a pair of sunglasses with a built-in audio-video recorder that she found online for under $300. She wasn't sure Alec would appreciate learning what she'd done with his money, though. Not that it was his any longer. And not that she was likely to tell him.

If he ever speaks to me again. She knew she'd acted like a jerk, turning down his offer of friendship, but where could it lead, really? She didn't fit. Wasn't the right woman. Had failed when he needed her most.

Thursday was her brother's twenty-seventh birthday. That evening she placed an internet call to him at Fort Campbell, Kentucky, where he was stationed. Amazing how grown-up her kid brother looked, with his blond hair shorter than she remembered and his gray eyes, a shade darker than her own, lighting up as he talked about his new girlfriend.

"I'm thinking of asking her to marry me," he said, his image remarkably clear on the screen in her home office. "Can you believe it? Me!"

"Congrats," she told him. "I've already got a tuxedo, so feel free to invite me to the wedding."

That sparked a laugh. "You're first on my list."

Without pausing to think, she blurted, "When Grandpa was alive, did you ever feel you were good enough for him?"

"Where did that come from?" he asked.

"Just wondering." Patty supposed it was a stupid question. She wasn't even sure why she'd asked it.

To her relief, Drew responded seriously. "No. I always wished I was like you."

Now there was a shock. "You think he considered *me* good enough? The way I kept messing up?"

"That's not what he told me," her brother responded. "He used to ask why I couldn't be as smart and hardworking as my sister."

"He did?"

"Of course, he only talked that way when you weren't around."

"Glad I have a brother to tell me these things."

They reminisced about Grandpa's backhanded approach to discipline and how he used to insist they make their beds so tightly he could bounce a coin on the sheets. "When I got to boot camp, it felt kind of familiar," Drew added.

"Yeah. Police academy was a breeze. Well, some of it." Patty actually felt nostalgic about the Sergeant and his old-fashioned methods, now that she was able to put them in perspective, with her brother for support.

At last the conversation tapered off. "I love you," she said. "Have the happiest birthday ever."

"You, too. I mean, thanks."

After ending the call, she sat staring at her computer. She might as well have an image of Grandpa as a screen saver, because she could see his face very clearly, wearing one of his rare smiles of approval. Too bad they'd never been quite enough to erase all that disappointment.

Maybe that was why she expected herself to be perfect, when there wasn't a perfect human being on earth. Not even Alec.

Alec. Lord, she missed him. But she wasn't ready to return his phone calls. Not yet.

Instead, she put in a call to Bailey. "Hey," Patty said when her friend answered. "I need your help."

On Saturday afternoon, Patty fumbled with her phone and nearly dropped it before her nervous fingers hit the right button. When Alec answered, she said without preamble, "Could you come over to my house in an hour?"

In the moment of silence that followed, she reflected that she should at least have identified herself. She might have also asked how everyone was doing, and made polite chitchat. Would she ever develop social graces?

"I'll be there," he answered, in that dear, familiar voice. "Should I bring anything special?"

"Like what?" she asked.

"Body armor? Clay pigeons?"

"Just yourself." Patty clicked off and then realized she hadn't said goodbye. Should she call him back? Oh, right. That *would* be awkward. *"Hi. Just wanted to say goodbye. So, bye."*

An hour. She'd better hurry.

In the bedroom, she took out two dresses she'd bought yesterday while shopping with Bailey. Real dresses. Two of them. One blue, one green. They were both cut low enough to show that she had breasts and high enough to show that she had legs. Bailey had assured her both were flattering without looking cheap.

Panty hose, high heels, a spritz of perfume that Bailey had helped her select. Good thing Patty already had the new hairstyle.

"I feel like your fairy godmother," her friend had chirped. She'd been in a buoyant mood all evening, thanks to the fact that her sister and brother-in-law had finally made up for sticking her with some bills. A rental house they owned had become vacant, and they'd promised to let her live there rent-free during the pregnancy.

In the bathroom, Patty applied the makeup she'd bought at a department-store cosmetics counter, where the saleslady had been happy to pick out this year's colors and show her the latest application techniques. In return, of course, for selling her a slew of wildly overpriced merchandise.

Worth every penny, Patty decided as she stepped back to regard her image. Oh, wait! She'd forgotten.

In the bedroom, she rummaged through a bureau drawer until she found the red-and-black thong panties she'd won at Nora's bridal shower, and changed into them. They felt weird, but gave her confidence. Reminded her she was just as much a woman as Sabrina or anybody else.

The doorbell rang.

Heart pounding, Patty jumped up and half ran to answer, nearly tripping in her three-inch heels. After a deep breath, she flung open the door.

And stared in dismay at the clot of beefy guys standing there. Bill Sanchez. George Green. Captain Reed. Leo. And Mike.

"Say what?" she asked.

Leo let out a wolf whistle. "Never thought you'd get this dressed up for our big match." In he clumped, followed by the others, laden with six-packs of beer, bags of pretzels and chips and cartons of dip. They didn't seem to notice, or care, that Patty practically had to cartwheel backward to get out of their way. "You clean up great, by the way."

"Nobody told me our match was today," she protested.

"Didn't you get the email?" George asked. "Too busy jumping off rooftops and tackling soap opera stars, I guess."

No use arguing that she always checked her business email account but let the personal one slide. "I have plans."

"You defaulting?" Leo waggled an eyebrow.

"No way!" She couldn't back down. They'd never let her forget it. "You're on."

The bell rang again. Cheeks flaming, Patty went to the door.

A bouquet of roses in hand, Alec stood there wearing a crisply pressed sport shirt, body-hugging jeans and an expression of pure hope. "Wow, you're a knockout." At a noise from behind her, he blinked. "You throwing a party?"

"They just showed up. It's that stupid bet I made about beating Leo at pool." Patty reached for the bouquet and held it to her nose. Only the faintest trace of a scent, but it filled her with joy.

She heard footsteps from behind. "You aren't going to bat that one away?" Mike teased.

"Not in a million years," Patty said.

A slow grin spread across Alec's face. "Is it too late to place my bet on you?"

Her heart squeezed. "Absolutely not."

PATTY WOULD HAVE HAVE WON the match if she hadn't stumbled in those annoying high heels and missed a bank shot. But she refused to make excuses.

"You win, fair and square," she told Leo. "But we're scheduling a rematch, and next time, I'm gonna teach you a few things."

"Big words," he hooted, and cheerfully took her twenty-dollar bill.

"Guess that's our cue to make ourselves scarce," said Mike, casting a meaningful glance at George and Bill, who were racking the balls for another game.

"Aw, come on." But George complied without further protest.

"And clean up your chips on the way out," Patty added. "I've got my own junk food."

"I'm taking the beer," said Bill.

"I didn't mean that."

"Too late."

Finally they were gone, leaving only a scattering of crumbs, a half-eaten container of dip and a few empty beer cans littering the den. Ignoring the mess, Patty took Alec's hand and led him into the living room.

The place didn't appeal to her the way it used to, she realized as they sat on her lumpy couch. The big-screen TV, easy-to-clean linoleum floor and scarred thrift-store furniture had been convenient, but there was something to be said for soothing colors and soft textures. On the coffee table, the roses leaned every which way in their oversize jar.

"I guess it's time I grew up," Patty mused.

"I love you the way you are." His hands cupping hers, Alec regarded her fiercely. "There isn't anything about you I don't love."

He'd said he loved her. Patty swallowed hard. Before she could respond, she had to explain. "The reason I called... I shouldn't have run away last Sunday. You deserve a second chance. And then some."

Alec's mouth twisted ruefully. "I was a complete idiot back in high school. I should have trusted my feelings and held on to you for all I was worth."

"You hurt me." Tears burned, and for a moment Patty could hear Grandpa scolding her about being one of those weak women who gave in to their emotions. But her feelings for Alec didn't make her weak. They filled her with strength. "Listen—"

"I'm sorry—" he said at the same time.

"Oh, quit apologizing and kiss me," she said, and pulled him close.

The kiss nearly melted her panty hose. She'd have liked a lot more, but something rustled in his shirt pocket, and he drew back.

"Hold on." He extracted a folded piece of paper and gave it to her. "I'm hoping we can skip the whole courtship business, since we already did that, and go right to the important part."

Wondering, Patty opened the sheet. It was a child's drawing of a ring with a lopsided diamond on top.

"I didn't have time to buy a real ring after you called," Alec explained, "so I asked Fiona to draw one. I didn't tell her what it was for, in case you turned me down. I just said I thought you'd like it."

Her throat clamped so tightly Patty couldn't speak. She'd once asked Bailey what it took to make a marriage work, but she'd had to discover the answer for herself. You needed to be friends and trust each other. You should feel happy together. And you had to be willing to throw yourself off a balcony and know that he'd catch you.

"Patty Hartman, will you marry me?" Alec asked.

"I guess I better," she said, "because you're the only man I've ever loved or ever will."

"Thank you."

"You're welcome."

They both started to laugh. When Alec held out his arms, Patty snuggled right up to him with a wonderful, warm, tingly feeling that told her this was right where she belonged.

Twelve years after the dance, she'd come home at last.

* * * * *

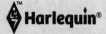
Harlequin®

American ★ Romance®

COMING NEXT MONTH

Available July 12, 2011

#1361 THE TEXAN AND THE COWGIRL
American Romance's Men of the West
Victoria Chancellor

#1362 THE COWBOY'S BONUS BABY
Callahan Cowboys
Tina Leonard

#1363 HER COWBOY DADDY
Texas Legacies: The McCabes
Cathy Gillen Thacker

#1364 THE BULL RIDER'S SECRET
Rodeo Rebels
Marin Thomas

You can find more information on upcoming
Harlequin® titles, free excerpts and more at
www.HarlequinInsideRomance.com.

REQUEST YOUR FREE BOOKS!

2 FREE NOVELS PLUS 2 FREE GIFTS!

♦ Harlequin®

American ★ Romance®

LOVE, HOME & HAPPINESS

YES! Please send me 2 FREE Harlequin American Romance® novels and my 2 FREE gifts (gifts are worth about \$10). After receiving them, if I don't wish to receive any more books, I can return the shipping statement marked "cancel." If I don't cancel, I will receive 4 brand-new novels every month and be billed just \$4.24 per book in the U.S. or \$4.99 per book in Canada. That's a saving of at least 15% off the cover price! It's quite a bargain! Shipping and handling is just 50¢ per book in the U.S. and 75¢ per book in Canada.* I understand that accepting the 2 free books and gifts places me under no obligation to buy anything. I can always return a shipment and cancel at any time. Even if I never buy another book, the two free books and gifts are mine to keep forever.

154/354 HDN FDKS

Name   (PLEASE PRINT)

Address   Apt. #

City   State/Prov.   Zip/Postal Code

Signature (if under 18, a parent or guardian must sign)

Mail to the **Reader Service:**
IN U.S.A.: P.O. Box 1867, Buffalo, NY 14240-1867
IN CANADA: P.O. Box 609, Fort Erie, Ontario L2A 5X3

Not valid for current subscribers to Harlequin American Romance books.

Want to try two free books from another line?
Call 1-800-873-8635 or visit www.ReaderService.com.

* Terms and prices subject to change without notice. Prices do not include applicable taxes. Sales tax applicable in N.Y. Canadian residents will be charged applicable taxes. Offer not valid in Quebec. This offer is limited to one order per household. All orders subject to credit approval. Credit or debit balances in a customer's account(s) may be offset by any other outstanding balance owed by or to the customer. Please allow 4 to 6 weeks for delivery. Offer available while quantities last.

Your Privacy—The Reader Service is committed to protecting your privacy. Our Privacy Policy is available online at www.ReaderService.com or upon request from the Reader Service.

We make a portion of our mailing list available to reputable third parties that offer products we believe may interest you. If you prefer that we not exchange your name with third parties, or if you wish to clarify or modify your communication preferences, please visit us at www.ReaderService.com/consumerschoice or write to us at Reader Service Preference Service, P.O. Box 9062, Buffalo, NY 14269. Include your complete name and address.

HARI I

USA TODAY *bestselling author B.J. Daniels
takes you on a trip to Whitehorse, Montana,
and the Chisholm Cattle Company.*

RUSTLED

Available July 2011 from Harlequin Intrigue.

As the dust settled, Dawson got his first good look at the rustler. A pair of big Montana sky-blue eyes glared up at him from a face framed by blond curls.

A woman rustler?

"You have to let me go," she hollered as the roar of the stampeding cattle died off in the distance.

"So you can finish stealing my cattle? I don't think so." Dawson jerked the woman to her feet.

She reached for the gun strapped to her hip hidden under her long barn jacket.

He grabbed the weapon before she could, his eyes narrowing as he assessed her. "How many others are there?" he demanded, grabbing a fistful of her jacket. "I think you'd better start talking before I tear into you."

She tried to fight him off, but he was on to her tricks and pinned her to the ground. He was suddenly aware of the soft curves beneath the jean jacket she wore under her coat.

"You have to listen to me." She ground out the words from between her gritted teeth. "You have to let me go. If you don't they will come back for me and they will kill you. There are too many of them for you to fight off alone. You won't stand a chance and I don't want your blood on my hands."

"I'm touched by your concern for me. Especially after you just tried to pull a gun on me."

"I wasn't going to shoot you."

Dawson hauled her to her feet and walked her the rest of the way to his horse. Reaching into his saddlebag, he pulled out a length of rope.

"You can't tie me up."

He pulled her hands behind her back and began to tie her wrists together.

"If you let me go, I can keep them from coming back," she said. "You have my word." She let out an unladylike curse. "I'm just trying to save your sorry neck."

"And I'm just going after my cattle."

"Don't you mean your boss's cattle?"

"Those cattle are mine."

"*You're* a Chisholm?"

"Dawson Chisholm. And you are…?"

"Everyone calls me Jinx."

He chuckled. "I can see why."

*Bronco busting, falling in love…it's all in a day's work.
Look for the rest of their story in*

RUSTLED

*Available July 2011 from Harlequin Intrigue
wherever books are sold.*